Angela, Private Citizen

Other Scholastic books
by Nancy K. Robinson

Oh Honestly, Angela!
Veronica Knows Best
Veronica the Show-off
Mom, You're Fired

Angela,
Private Citizen

Nancy K. Robinson

SCHOLASTIC HARDCOVER

Scholastic Inc.
New York

Grateful acknowledgment is made for permission to reprint an excerpt from *Hansel and Gretel* retold by Ruth Belov Gross. Text copyright © 1988 by Ruth Belov Gross.

Library of Congress Cataloging-in-Publication Data

Robinson, Nancy K.
  Angela, private citizen.
  Summary: Six-year-old Angela's faith in order and fairness is frequently shaken as she tries to cope with all the mysteries of life that keep turning up in her busy family.
  [1. Family life—Fiction]   I. Title.
PZ7.R56754An   1989   [Fic]   89-5918

ISBN 0-590-41726-6

12 11 10 9 8 7 6 5 4 3 2 1   9/8 0 1 2 3 4/9

Printed in the U.S.A.   37
First Scholastic printing, November 1989

*To John Cederquist whom Angela has
always found worthy of her trust . . .*

Contents

Angela's Income Tax   1

A Contribution to Science   13

Filling In the Blanks   25

Pinwheel Power   29

Cleaning Up   35

The Long Arm of the Law   40

The Right Type   49

A Bowl of Cherries   63

Vacation Plans   77

Bedtime Story   87

Other Arrangements   95

Sentence Fun   104

A Visit to the Post Office   108

Sweet Potato Salad and
    Chocolate Graham Cake   120

The Plot Unfolds . . .   129

Out of the Woods   135

Angela, Private Citizen

Angela's Income Tax

It was Saturday morning, the fifteenth of April. Angela was the first one awake. She tiptoed through the apartment. Something very important was going on in the Steele household.

The dining room table was cluttered with bills, receipts, envelopes and impressive-looking forms and booklets.

For a whole week Angela's family had been forced to eat every meal in the kitchen. Her mother and father had been tired and cross. They hardly ever fought, but Angela heard them snapping at each other a few times. She knew it was only because they were working so hard. It would all be over tonight.

Angela was in a holiday mood. "Today is Income Tax Day!" she whispered happily. Her father had told her that the income tax forms had to be mailed by midnight.

Angela felt she was part of something very exciting. She was proud that her family was helping the United States government, and she did her best to help, too.

All week long she had tried to protect her mother and father. She didn't want them to be disturbed by anything.

Every time the telephone rang, Angela ran to answer it. Everyone in the family let her do it until they found out *how* she was answering the phone.

It didn't matter if the caller was a friend or someone offering her father extra work as a musician, Angela answered the phone the same way:

"Hello. No one can talk to you. Guess what! Income tax! 'Bye."

"Everyone has to do their income tax," her older sister Tina told her. "It's not exactly the most thrilling thing in the world."

"Maybe it is and maybe it isn't."

Angela was six years old now. She was old enough to know Tina could be wrong about some things. "The government really needs our money, and I hope we have plenty left over to give them."

"Oh honestly, Angela!" Tina had groaned. "You don't understand anything. First of all, no one *likes* to pay income tax. And secondly, you don't pay everything that's left over. You pay a *percentage* of your total income."

"What's a *percentage?*" Angela had wanted to know.

"It's much too complicated to explain," Tina had said, "especially to a first-grader."

"Well, anyway," Angela had shrugged, "I hope we pay the government lots and lots of *percentage.*"

Angela had been worried about the state of the nation's treasury ever since February. One Saturday afternoon, she had gone with her family to hear her older brother, Nathaniel, in a debate. The topic was the national debt.

RESOLVED: That the size of the national debt is harmful to future generations.

Angela was proud of Nathaniel. He had to argue that it wasn't harmful, even though he thought it was, and his team had won the debate!

The following Monday, when her first grade had their weekly discussion, "The World Around Us," Angela had raised her hand and told her class the shocking news: The country was spending more money than it had in the bank!

Miss Mason had smiled, nodded and said, "Thank you, Angela. That is certainly a big concern to everyone."

But none of her classmates believed her. Meredith had screeched with laughter. Chris told her at lunchtime that it wasn't true and she'd "better shut up." And Cheryl White said that if Angela ever said that again, she would tell the school nurse.

"Tell her, then," Angela said bravely.

(Cheryl White was forever reporting people to the school nurse. If Cheryl fell down and scraped her own knee — someone made her do it! Someone else always got blamed.)

Angela tried to be very quiet when her parents were working on their taxes. She tried to stop Tina and Nathaniel from slamming doors.

There had been a lot of door-slamming lately.

Tina was twelve and Nathaniel was fourteen. They always seemed to be fighting. These fights usually ended with both of them going to their rooms and slamming the doors.

"I guess it's the age," their mother would sigh.

"Nonsense," Angela heard her father say in a tight voice. He played the cello in the city orchestra, but for the past few months he had been taking extra jobs at weddings and school dances. There were lots of bills to pay. He needed quiet and sleep very badly.

But Tina and Nathaniel slammed doors for other reasons, too. They each said they "needed their privacy."

Angela thought it sounded very grand to "need privacy." She wished that she needed some of that, too, but she kept the door to her tiny room open all the time. She kept hoping Tina or Nathaniel would drop in for a little visit — the way they used to in "olden days."

To Angela, "olden days" was a time in the far distant past, when Tina and Nathaniel didn't fight so much — when they had more time for Angela.

But this morning the apartment was quiet. Everyone was still asleep. Angela climbed up on

5

a chair next to the dining room table and looked over the papers. She looked longingly at one of the booklets, which was called Taxpayer's Form 1040.

This was her favorite. She wanted one just like it. Very carefully Angela turned the pages of the form. She enjoyed looking at the blanks and boxes to be filled out, just like in her first-grade reading workbook, . . . "but without the pictures, of course," Angela told herself.

Angela loved workbooks. Not everyone in Miss Mason's first-grade class shared her fondness for them. Eddie Bishop, her reading partner, hated workbooks.

Eddie always got upset trying to figure out the questions. He always suspected a trick. Sometimes he just gave up and sat staring out the window, leaving the whole page blank.

Angela knew Eddie could read, but no one else did. Even Miss Mason did not know Eddie could read. "Give it your best try," she would whisper to Eddie, but, when Eddie tried, he got every answer wrong.

The Form 1040 workbook looked quite difficult. Angela wondered if that was the reason her parents hadn't started filling it out yet.

It suddenly occurred to her that it might be an extra copy. They might not be using it.

Not only did Angela *want* a Form 1040; she *needed* one.

Angela had a nice surprise for the federal government. She was going to pay taxes, too! She knew the government needed every cent it could get.

She had saved $4.53 since Christmas, and she could just imagine how pleased the President of the United States would be to get that money. All she needed was a nice Form 1040 to send in along with it. It had a place for her name and address and lots of "fill-in-the-blanks."

Angela got thirty-five cents a week for pocket money. In addition to this, she made extra money entertaining a cat in the building when the owners went away each weekend.

It was not exactly *her* job. The job of feeding the cat belonged to a ten-year-old girl named Madeline who lived on the first floor.

But Madeline was afraid of the cat, whose name was Moxie, so she paid Angela twenty-five cents a weekend to hold her hand when she entered the apartment, find out where Moxie was hiding so that Moxie would not jump out and scare her, and to entertain Moxie by petting her and talking to her.

Madeline did not want Moxie to get "psy-cat-trick" problems, as she called them.

Angela had one big expense. Everyone in her family contributed to the support of an orphan named Flor Elena through the Rescue the Children program. Flor Elena lived in another country, but Angela could never remember the name of the country. Every month the Steele family contributed $17 to help Flor Elena.

Each month Angela put in fifty cents.

Her wealth had increased slightly one cold January day, when she found three pennies on the sidewalk on the way home from school.

Angela took a deep breath and turned the page of Form 1040.

"Angela! What are you doing?"

Tina was standing behind her with a frightened expression on her face.

Tina was already dressed, and Angela thought she looked very pretty. She was wearing a blue denim skirt and a pink sweatshirt. Under the sweatshirt she was wearing a white blouse with the collar turned up. Her hair had been carefully blown dry.

Angela was surprised. Tina and Nathaniel usually slept late on weekends. Then she remembered that Nathaniel's best friend Doug was sleeping over. She had noticed that Tina always tried to look nice when Doug was around.

"Don't touch that form!" Tina said.

"I was only looking." Angela closed the booklet and tucked her hands behind her back.

Tina looked over Angela's shoulder at the form. "Oh, no!" Tina said miserably. "They haven't even begun filling it out yet. I told Melissa I'd let her know this morning if I can go to Camp Sunset this summer."

Angela felt sorry for her sister. Tina had spent hours dreaming over the brochures of Camp Sunset. More than anything she wanted to be a Sunset girl just like her friend, Melissa Glenn — but she hadn't gotten up the nerve to ask Melissa how much the camp cost. And she hadn't said a word yet to her parents.

Tina was staring at the form. "I wanted to wait

until they finished their taxes," she muttered.

Suddenly Tina leaned forward and looked more closely at Form 1040.

"Oh, no wonder!" she said with relief. "It's last year's form."

Angela looked at the year at the top of the form. "That's last year's, all right," Angela said happily. The first grade had been made well aware of the new year and the new calendar when they returned from their Christmas vacation in January.

"Well," Angela said, "I guess they won't be needing this."

"They might," Tina said vaguely. "You'd better leave it alone."

"But it's last year's," Angela said.

Tina wasn't paying attention. She had heard a noise somewhere in the apartment. Suddenly she gasped and ran to the front hall mirror.

Angela climbed down from the chair and followed her.

"Nathaniel and Doug are up!" Tina stared at herself in the mirror. "I look terrible."

"No, you don't," Angela said. "You look nice."

"This sweatshirt is too tight," Tina mumbled. "I'm changing."

"It looks nice," Angela said.

"Don't lie to me," Tina said crossly.

Angela felt hurt, but she followed Tina down the hall.

"Tina," she whispered, "do you think Mommy and Daddy need that workbook?"

Tina didn't seem to hear her.

"Tina . . ."

Tina whirled around.

"Angela, don't you see I'm busy?"

Tina went into her room and slammed the door.

Angela stood in the hallway looking up at the signs Tina had recently posted on her door:

DO NOT ENTER

PRIVATE PROPERTY   KEEP OUT

NO TRESPASSING — AND THIS MEANS YOU!

" . . . and don't slam doors," Angela called softly.

But there was no answer.

Angela went back to the living room and climbed up on the chair.

"Well," she said out loud, "I guess no one will be needing this old thing." She looked around. Then she stared at Form 1040. "It's last year's,

11

all right," she said, nodding with satisfaction.

After a while she said, "They're just going to throw it away."

There was no one to argue with her, so Angela picked up the form and took it to her room.

She put it on her white worktable and took out her piggy bank, her box of crayons and colored pencils which she kept in a small chest.

She took out her envelope stuffed with decorative stickers.

Then, for the first time ever, Angela closed the door to her room.

She settled down at her desk to give Taxpayer's Form 1040 "her best try."

A Contribution
to Science

On the way to the kitchen Tina passed Angela's room and was surprised to see the door was closed. There was a sign. BISY, it read. Tina smiled and went to help Nathaniel fix breakfast in the kitchen.

Their parents were back at work on their taxes. Tina was sorry they couldn't eat at the dining room table. It would be crowded in the kitchen.

Nathaniel was stirring the pancake batter. His friend Doug was sitting at the kitchen table making a list on a legal pad.

"Tina!" Doug said. "Just the person we were waiting for."

Tina felt herself blush. She went to the refrigerator and took out the container of orange juice.

"What do you mean?" Tina asked.

Tina didn't think it was very civilized to serve the orange juice in a plastic container so she searched through the cupboard until she found an ironstone jug with bright blue flowers on it. It had been one of her parents' wedding presents. She rinsed it out and poured the juice into it.

Nathaniel groaned. "What are you doing that for? We'll just have to wash it."

"I'll wash it," Tina mumbled. She hoped Doug wouldn't think they were a bunch of barbarians.

"We really need your help," Doug said.

Tina was pleased. "On the science project?" she asked.

Doug nodded. "We still haven't picked what we're going to do."

Nathaniel and Doug were in the ninth grade. Tina was in seventh, but they all went to the same junior high school. There was going to be a science fair in the school gym the first week in June. Ever since the third grade Nathaniel and Doug had worked together on science projects. They set very high standards for themselves.

"What happened to your idea of building a time machine?" Tina asked. She had been very interested in that idea. She had thought it would be fun to learn history by propelling herself back in time. It would be a lot easier and far more exciting than going to the library.

"Mr. Krull won't let us do it," her brother told her. "He wouldn't even look at our plans."

"Why not?" Tina asked.

"He called the idea 'science fiction fantasy,' " Nathaniel grumbled. "You see, he doesn't want us to do anything interesting."

Tina nodded. Two weeks ago Nathaniel had come home from school furious that their science teacher, Mr. Krull, wouldn't even let them try to create life in a test tube.

"Just because scientists haven't done it yet is no reason for him not to even give us a chance." Nathaniel was quite bitter.

"Life in a test tube?" their father had asked in a mild voice. "Aren't scientists pretty far away from being able to do that?"

"Look, Dad." Nathaniel sounded a little annoyed. "Mr. Krull would be happy if we did something really boring, like the Life Cycle of a Green

Plant. Doug and I want to do something important. We want to make a contribution to science."

At the time Tina had noticed that both her parents seemed to be having trouble eating. They each found an excuse to leave the table.

Nathaniel became suspicious and was shocked to find his mother and father in the kitchen doubled over with laughter.

Without a word, he had gone to his room and slammed the door. Tina hadn't blamed him a bit. From that moment on, Nathaniel had refused to discuss the science project in their parents' presence.

Tina sat down at the table to let Nathaniel and Doug know she would give the matter her full attention — that she, at least, took them seriously.

"What are some of your ideas?" she asked.

Doug looked at the list and cleared his throat. "We were thinking of developing a cure for the common cold."

"That sounds good," Tina said. "Why don't you go ahead and do that?"

"Mr. Krull won't let us," Nathaniel told her. "He rejected that idea, too."

"How ridiculous!" Tina said hotly. "People need

a cure for the common cold. Doesn't Mr. Krull trust you to do *anything*?"

She was pleased to see that Doug was smiling at her.

"I know," Nathaniel said. "And now we're afraid he's going to reject our best idea of all."

"What's that?" Tina asked.

Doug looked at Nathaniel. Then he leaned over and said quietly, "We want to create a model of a black hole."

"Wouldn't that be fantastic?" Nathaniel asked.

"I guess so." Tina felt confused. "But what's a black hole?"

Nathaniel sighed, but Doug said patiently, "It's a star that has collapsed on itself. The mass has become so dense and the force of gravity is so strong that nothing can escape."

"Not even light," Nathaniel said. "That's why it appears black."

Tina was having trouble picturing such a thing. She wondered how honest she should be.

"Well," she said slowly, "there's no doubt about it. Creating a black hole in the school gym would be very . . . um . . . dramatic. . . ."

"It sure would be!" Nathaniel said. "Of course,"

he added, "we'd have lots of boring charts and diagrams to go along with it."

" . . . but," Tina went on, "is there such a thing? Are there really black holes in space?"

"Yes," Doug said quickly. "Well, in theory, I guess. No one has actually discovered one yet, but they have to be there."

"Oh," Tina said. Nathaniel and Doug seemed very discouraged. They were quiet for a few minutes. Finally Doug said, "Tina's right. Too theoretical."

"I know," Nathaniel said unhappily. "Mr. Krull will say 'no.' We're just wasting our time. Besides, there are a few things we haven't worked out."

"Tina," Doug said. "We need new ideas. Fresh ideas."

The three of them sat at the kitchen table thinking hard. Half an hour went by and all they could think of was a couple of diseases that needed cures.

There were a few interruptions. Their mother came in to find out when breakfast would be ready.

"Any minute," Nathaniel told her.

Their father came in to fix himself a cup of coffee. "How's the science project coming?" he asked.

"Everything's under control," Nathaniel told him a little abruptly.

Then Angela appeared, wanting to know what the word "spouse" meant.

"A husband if you're the wife; a wife if you're the husband," Tina told her.

Right after that Melissa called wanting to know if Tina had asked her parents about Camp Sunset yet.

"I'm about to," Tina said. "Oh, by the way," she asked casually, "how much does it cost?"

"I don't know," Melissa said. "It couldn't be that much. There's not even electricity in the cabins."

Tina felt uneasy, but she promised to call Melissa as soon as she asked her parents.

Angela was back in the kitchen. "What if you're not a husband or a wife? What if you're a sister?"

Tina sighed. "Then you're not a spouse. Angela, can't you see we're busy?"

"I'm busy, too," Angela said sadly.

"Go ask Mommy and Daddy," Tina said.

19

Angela went into the dining room, but her mother and father were in the middle of an argument. It was a polite argument.

"Well," her father was saying, "I'd feel a lot better if we looked for it right now."

"Don't be silly," her mother said. "It's somewhere around. We're nowhere near ready to fill it out. We have to add up every single one of these piles of paper. It will take hours. I'll look for it when we take a break."

"I would still feel a lot better . . ."

Angela tiptoed back to her room. She hated polite arguments. She thought polite arguments were worse than the screaming kind.

It was quiet in the kitchen. Tina, Nathaniel, and Doug had even run out of diseases that needed cures. Tina sat at the table gazing out the window at the rain.

It was a blustery day. Gusts of wind blew the trees that lined the sidewalk.

Down below, Tina saw a man chasing a yellow-and-green striped umbrella. It rolled over and over — a bright blur of color.

Tina felt she was getting the beginning of an idea. . . .

"Listen," Tina said, "I was thinking . . . you know how everyone talks about finding alternate sources of energy. Ways of creating electricity without using up valuable resources or polluting the atmosphere. . . ."

"If you're going to say solar power," Nathaniel said, "forget it. Everyone does solar power."

"Not solar power," Tina said.

"Tidal power?" Doug asked. "Ocean currents? Harnessing volcanic energy?"

"Wind power," Tina said. "Using the wind to generate electricity."

"I always liked the idea of windmill power," Doug said thoughtfully. "It's quiet. No pollution, either."

"We only have ten dollars in our budget," Nathaniel said. "Building a windmill would be pretty expensive."

Tina was thinking about the umbrella. She giggled. "I was thinking of something more like a pinwheel. . . ."

Nathaniel was staring at Tina. Suddenly he

jumped to his feet and began pacing up and down the narrow kitchen. "Not just one pinwheel," he muttered to himself. "A whole bunch of pinwheels. A field of pinwheels blowing in the breeze — making enough electricity to light . . . to light . . ."

"My dollhouse!" Tina said. "You could use my old dollhouse. The electric bulbs are still in it."

"Pinwheel power?" Doug grinned. "Pinwheel power. I like that idea!" He sat thinking for a moment and then began making sketches on the legal pad. "Look," he said, "if we attach a ring of balsa wood to the back of each pinwheel with a groove around it, we could connect it to a pulley with a rubber band. . . ."

Doug had always been the practical one of the team.

Nathaniel didn't have time to look at the sketches. He was too excited. "I have a feeling this is just what the public is looking for. . . ."

Nathaniel began describing a vision of the future . . . town after town converting to pinwheel power. "Gardens, window boxes, meadows full of pinwheels, like tulips lining the highways across the entire country. . . ."

"We can buy quite a lot of pinwheels for ten dollars," Doug added. "Tina, you're a genius."

Tina felt like a genius, but she said modestly, "Well, it's just an idea. . . ."

"It's fantastic!" her brother said. "Tina, I just want you to know, you will get credit for this."

Tina blushed. All at once she saw a career for herself as a city planner. She was thinking of all the nice outfits she would wear when she made her presentations.

"I'll need eyeglasses," she told herself, "so that people respect my opinions. . . . Delicate tortoiseshell frames and a gray tint to the glass. . . ." Melissa's mother had a pair like that. She called them her theater glasses.

"We've got to get started right away," Nathaniel said.

"My dollhouse could use a fresh coat of paint," Tina said.

"I'll go buy the pinwheels," Doug said.

"There are some old window boxes around here," Nathaniel said. "We can put the pinwheels in window boxes."

As they were making the list, Tina noticed that her mother had come into the kitchen. She seemed to be looking for something.

She even went poking through the kitchen garbage pail, which Tina found very embarrassing — especially with Doug sitting right there.

"I'll look for it later," her mother muttered. "It couldn't have gone far."

Filling In
the Blanks

Angela had colored in most of the squares on the form. It made a pretty design. She had filled in her name and address and had changed the year to bring it up to date.

After much thought, she crossed out the word *Spouse* and wrote SISTER TO TINA AND NATHANIEL on the lines below. Certainly the government would be interested in knowing a little about her.

But most of Form 1040 puzzled her. She had finally decided that the most important part was the money the government needed, so she taped all her quarters and pennies onto a piece of cardboard. She stuck the cardboard into the big envelope she had addressed to the President of the United States.

In the left-hand corner she wrote her name and address so that the President would know where to send the thank-you note.

It seemed a little heavy, so Angela put all twenty stamps her grandmother had sent her on the envelope.

Her grandmother had sent her those stamps and a nice box of stationery in the hopes that Angela would write her a few letters, but Angela was sure her grandmother would understand that paying income tax was more important.

Of course Angela was deeply distressed about the national debt. She found it embarrassing that the government had to borrow money.

But she was even more concerned about her reading partner, Eddie Bishop.

Two weeks ago, Eddie had come to school without his milk money. Angela had overheard Eddie telling Miss Mason that his grandmother's social security check had not arrived from the government yet.

Miss Mason told him not to worry about the

milk money. "Bring it when you can," she told Eddie. But Angela noticed that Eddie refused to take a carton of milk at lunchtime and sat very stiffly in his seat for the rest of the day.

Angela could not sleep that night. She was afraid the government had run out of money before they remembered to write the check to Eddie's grandmother. She was relieved when Eddie brought his milk money the next day.

Eddie lived with his grandmother and his brothers and sisters in a run-down building behind the school. It didn't seem fair to Angela that everyone could see how poor his family was right from the schoolyard.

Eddie never had new clothes. He wore hand-me-downs that never fit properly. But what bothered Angela the most was the way Eddie's hair smelled. It didn't smell dirty. It smelled too clean. It smelled like disinfectant or Lysol. Other kids noticed it, too. Cheryl White sometimes held her nose when Eddie was around.

"How can you stand being Eddie's reading partner?" she once asked Angela. "How can you stand the smell?"

Angela made up her mind that the most important issue facing the country was making it possible for people like Eddie's grandmother to buy real shampoo. She even considered writing a little note on the tax form, but there didn't seem to be a place for suggestions.

Angela was surprised the government didn't ask her how she wanted her $4.53 spent.

She sighed and turned back to the first page to admire her work.

Right at the top she had stuck a flag sticker surrounded by gold stars, blue stars and green stars. She had put a pretty rainbow sticker in each corner.

Angela was feeling a little disappointed that no one was knocking on her door trying to find out why she was so busy. She went to the door and took off her BISY sign. She left the door open and sat at her desk, hoping someone would pass by and happen to notice her paying her income tax.

She was beginning to feel a little hungry.

After a while, she gave up and went to the kitchen to see what was going on.

Pinwheel Power

"What happened to breakfast?"

Tina looked up from the dollhouse she was painting and saw her mother standing in the doorway.

"Where are the pancakes?" her mother asked.

"Oh, we thought pancakes would be too messy," Nathaniel said as he scooped some potting soil into a window box that was sitting on the kitchen counter.

"Too messy," their mother repeated, staring at the bag of dirt on the floor. She looked around at the newspapers on the floor. The kitchen table was covered with newspapers, too.

Angela was sitting at the table in her blue smock helping Tina paint the dollhouse. She had managed to get quite a lot of white paint on her face and in her hair. On the other hand, Tina's old dollhouse was beginning to look quite nice with a fresh coat of white paint.

Doug was using the counter next to the sink as a worktable. He was sanding down pieces of balsa wood.

"Too messy," their mother repeated.

"Yup," Nathaniel said. "Pancakes would be too messy. We all had cereal instead. How would you and Dad like a nice bowl of cereal delivered to you on a tray?"

"Don't worry, Mrs. Steele," Doug said. "We'll clean everything up."

But their mother was staring at the rows of shiny pinwheels lying on baking sheets on top of the stove.

"Science project?" she asked.

"Not just any science project," Nathaniel said.

"But why today?" his mother asked. "The science fair isn't until June."

Nathaniel seemed surprised and a little hurt at the question. "We have to let Mr. Krull know on

Monday. We have to test it out right away."

Jessica Steele watched the activity for a few minutes. Then she asked in a small voice, "Are you going to bake the pinwheels?"

Everyone laughed. Angela laughed the hardest of all. "Don't be silly, Mommy," she said. "We're going to plant the pinwheels. We're going to plant the pinwheels and grow electricity."

Angela was having the most wonderful Income Tax Day. She was delighted that she was allowed to help on the science project.

While the dollhouse was drying, she watched as Doug and Nathaniel hooked up the pinwheels to pulleys that were connected with rubber bands to a board full of nails and wires which Doug called the magnetic field.

Nathaniel placed the window boxes around the dollhouse on the kitchen table. Then he placed the pinwheels in the window boxes in shiny rows. Angela even got to "plant" a few pinwheels.

Angela sighed. "It's beautiful!"

"Not bad," Nathaniel said.

"The shutters don't look so great," Tina said. "I wish I had painted them, too."

Angela was especially happy that no one was fighting. The apartment was peaceful with everyone busy at work.

She served her parents a late lunch of bologna sandwiches on a tray.

The clicking noises of the calculator made a pleasant sound on a rainy afternoon. Angela stayed for a while and watched.

Her mother was calling off numbers while her father punched the keys. After he had added up each pile of receipts, her father tore off the piece of tape from the calculator and placed it carefully on top of that pile.

Angela decided that next year she would have lots of expenses, too. Maybe she would even ask for her own calculator for Christmas. . . .

"We really need paper clips," her father said. "We should clip the receipts to the totals."

"I'll get them!" Angela said, happy to be of even more help.

Just then there was a shout from the kitchen. "It's working!" Nathaniel shouted.

Angela ran to the kitchen.

To her amazement the little bulbs in Tina's dollhouse were flickering on and off. The kitchen window was open and gusts of wind were turning some of the pinwheels in the window boxes surrounding the dollhouse. But the wind wasn't steady enough to keep them turning.

Even so, every time the lights flickered on, Tina, Doug, and Nathaniel jumped up and down and cried, "We did it!"

"What a terrific idea!" Her father had come to see it, too. His face was flushed. He seemed just as excited as the children.

"Pinwheel power!" He laughed. "A step forward for mankind. How did you ever think of it?"

"It was Tina's idea," Nathaniel said. But he seemed very pleased that his father liked it. "There's just one problem. We can't seem to get the pinwheels to keep turning. We were thinking of using a fan. . . ."

"But," Doug said, "we would use more electricity than we are generating."

"We want it all to be natural," Nathaniel explained to his father.

"It *would* be a pity to use a fan. Let me see. . . ." Their father studied the problem.

Angela hoped he hadn't forgotten his income tax.

"You know," he said after a while, "I think the solution is simple. You can keep the pinwheels turning by creating a draft — a steady flow of air."

"But how?" Nathaniel asked.

"All you have to do is open a window in another room. Let me see. . . . Why don't you try opening the living room window first."

Nathaniel went to open it.

A moment later all the pinwheels were turning.

They did not start and stop; they kept turning. And the lights in the dollhouse stayed on.

Nathaniel was back. "You were right, Dad," he said happily. "Mom, come see!" he called.

But there was no answer.

"Mom, quick! You've got to see it!"

"Forget the taxes for a moment, Jessica!" his father shouted.

"I'll go get her," Angela volunteered.

She found her mother desperately trying to close the window. Little pieces of paper were floating around in the breeze. They looked like pieces of confetti.

The dining room table was bare.

Cleaning Up

It took the rest of the afternoon to collect the papers. Everyone helped, including Doug. Angela put paper clips on each pile.

At five o'clock Angela went with Madeline to help feed Moxie the cat. When she got back, her parents were tearing the apartment apart looking for something.

"Do you have to mail your income tax exactly at midnight?" Angela asked Tina, who was in the kitchen helping Nathaniel and Doug clean up.

"Of course not," Tina said. "You can mail it any time before midnight. But, if you miss the last pickup of mail from the mailbox at the corner, you have to take it down to the main post office. It has to be postmarked by midnight." She sighed. "I hope they don't have to do that. It takes a long time to get down there."

Angela wondered if she would be allowed to stay up until midnight on such a special day. But on New Year's Eve she had only been allowed to stay up until ten o'clock.

"What time do they pick up the mail at the corner?" Angela asked.

"At seven o'clock," Tina said.

It was five-thirty. Angela decided she would mail her income tax early. She went to her room to seal the envelope.

Doug had to go home. Tina said good-bye and blushed when Doug said, "Thanks again, Tina."

"You know, Tina," Nathaniel said when they were alone in the kitchen. (Their parents were still searching the apartment for something.) "I was thinking . . . maybe other toys could be used as sources of energy. You know, when kids are running around playing, they could also be doing something useful for society."

Tina was interested. After all, her career in city planning was off to a good start.

"What toys, for instance?" she asked.

"Maybe a yoyo," Nathaniel said.

"Yoyo power?" Tina asked.

Just then her mother burst into the kitchen.

"Look, kids," she said desperately. "Has anyone, by any chance, seen our 1040 form? We can't find it anyplace."

"Nope," Nathaniel said.

"Only last year's," Tina said.

"I don't understand what could have happened to it." Her mother seemed very upset, and went back to look.

"I don't understand how the yoyos could be hooked up to any . . . um . . . system . . ." Tina went on, "and would it really be *feasible* to — "

"Wait a minute!" Their mother was back. "Tina, did you say you saw last year's form?"

Tina nodded. "On the dining room table."

"Was it blank?" her mother asked.

Tina nodded again. "But it was for last year. It was out-of-date."

"It's always dated the previous year," her mother said. "We declare our income tax for the year before. That's the one we're looking for."

"Can I go to the mailbox by myself?" Angela was standing in the kitchen wearing her yellow slicker and red boots and carrying a manila envelope under her arm.

"Well, I guess so," her mother said. "If you promise to come right back."

"I promise," Angela said.

Angela stood there a moment hoping someone would ask her what the important envelope was, but her mother just turned back to Tina and said, "That's where I thought it was, too. On the dining room table. . . ."

Angela passed her father in the hallway. He was searching through a pile of magazines, looking for something.

"Where are you off to?" he asked Angela.

"To the mailbox," Angela said.

"By yourself?" her father asked.

"It's okay," Angela told him. "I already asked Mommy . . . I mean . . ." she corrected herself, "I already asked your spouse," and she went out the door.

Her father stood there a few seconds thinking.

"That's funny," he said to himself, "Angela just said 'spouse.'"

Angela felt very grown-up taking the elevator to the lobby by herself. She said "hello" to the doorman and gave him a moment to ask her what she was doing, but the intercom rang and he turned his back to answer it.

Angela tucked the envelope into her slicker and ran to the mailbox. She stood on tiptoes and pulled it open.

"Real shampoo for Eddie," she prayed and dropped the envelope in.

Suddenly Angela had a wonderful feeling. It didn't matter that nobody knew. She didn't need praise; she didn't need approval.

Angela skipped back to the lobby feeling very good inside. She pushed the elevator button and did a little dance as she waited.

The elevator door opened and her mother stepped out.

"Angela," she said in a quiet voice. "What did you just mail?"

Angela looked at her mother's face and the good feeling inside her disappeared.

The Long Arm
of the Law

"How could you do such a thing?" her mother wanted to know. "How could you take that form without asking?"

"You never send money through the mail," Tina told Angela. "You send a check. The computer won't have the faintest idea what to do with your income tax form."

"Besides," Nathaniel said, "you send your income tax to the Internal Revenue Service, not to the President of the United States."

"I told her not to touch that form," Tina said to her mother. "I told her again and again."

"You also told her it was last year's form," her mother said. "It's as much your fault as it is hers, Tina."

Tina was quiet and glared at Angela. She was in a bad mood. Melissa had just called again to find out about Camp Sunset, but Tina had decided this would not be the best time to ask her parents. "Can't talk right this minute," she had said breathlessly to Melissa. "Call you back, okay?"

Melissa didn't say "okay"; she just hung up.

"Well, it's too late now," her mother said. "All I can do is try to get to the main post office and see if there are any 1040 forms left. In this weather the buses will be slow. It will take over an hour just to get there, and another hour to get back." It was six o'clock.

"And then we'll have to fill it out, write out the checks and take it all the way down to the main post office again. We'll never make it by midnight." Angela's father didn't seem cross; he just seemed discouraged. "I have a concert tonight. I won't be back until ten-thirty."

"Why didn't you tell me you had a concert tonight?" his wife said angrily.

41

"If you'll remember correctly, I have a concert every Saturday night," her husband said in a cold, but even voice.

Angela held her breath praying that this would not be one of those polite fights, but her mother just said miserably, "I completely forgot today was Saturday." She was quiet for a moment. Then she said in a rush, "What if I go down, get the form, come back, fill it out and meet you down at Town Hall after the concert . . . then you go over it, sign it, we write the checks and both go down . . ." She had to stop; she had run out of breath.

"We'll never make it," her husband said. "They've probably run out of 1040 forms, anyway."

"Well, I think we should try."

Angela could not believe what a terrible thing she had done. She could not believe how much trouble she had caused.

"I suppose you thought it was cute," Tina said after their father and mother had gone.

Angela thought about the pretty rainbow stickers in each corner of the form and didn't say anything.

And when Angela tried to help wash the dishes, Tina said, "Never mind. You've done enough damage today."

"Oh, come on, Tina," Nathaniel said. "Leave her alone. Remember, Angela gave her life savings away today."

It was true. Angela had turned over every penny she had to help bail out the government. She had a feeling she was going to cost the country more than $4.53 in time and energy. "Maybe even break the computers," Tina had suggested casually.

Worst of all, her parents were in trouble.

"Big trouble," Tina said.

"What's going to happen to them?" Angela asked. "What happens if Mommy and Daddy don't get their taxes in on time?"

"Oh, the Internal Revenue Service comes after them," Tina said cheerfully. "That's all. They just grab Mom and Dad and lock them up in this special prison for a couple of years. Won't that be fun? And guess whose fault it is."

Angela's mouth fell open. She stared up at Tina.

"Don't tell her that, Tina," Nathaniel said. "Angela." He stooped down to talk to her, and she stared up at him with wide open eyes. "Mom and

Dad won't go to prison . . ." he began.

"What do you mean?" Tina said. "People go to prison all the time for not paying their taxes. It's in the news all the time."

"For evading their taxes," Nathaniel said, "for doing it on purpose. Why are you trying to scare Angela like that?"

"She deserves it," Tina said coldly. "She ought to know what a serious thing she did."

Angela didn't know who to believe. "What if the government thinks they did it on purpose?" she asked Nathaniel in a voice barely above a whisper.

"Look, Angela," Nathaniel said. "As long as they get it in, all they have to do is pay a fine for getting it in late."

"Great," Tina said, "they'll probably use up the money I need to go to Camp Sunset."

Angela spent the evening standing by the front door listening for the elevator. Every time she heard it moving, she opened the front door hoping the elevator would stop on her floor . . . hoping her mother would step out waving a brand-new 1040 form.

By eight-thirty her mother still hadn't returned.

Tina and Nathaniel were watching television, so Angela put herself to bed.

She tried very hard to stay awake, but she couldn't keep her eyes open.

Angela was dreaming about a goldfish — an enormous goldfish. It was so big it took up a whole fishbowl. But the tank was leaking. There was no water left. The goldfish was stuck in the tank gasping for air. . . .

Angela was trying to save the goldfish. She poured buckets of water into the bowl, but it all leaked out.

"Help, Tina!" she said, but Tina just stood there watching her. Tina's lips weren't moving, but Angela could hear her sister's voice in her ear saying, "I suppose you think that's cute," over and over and over again. . . .

Angela woke up with a start. It was morning.

She had an odd feeling. She was sure she was alone in the apartment.

She jumped out of bed and ran to her parents' bedroom. The door was wide open. The bed hadn't been slept in.

Do parents run away from home? she asked

herself. Do they run away from home to get away from children who are too much trouble?

She crossed the hall and stood in front of Tina's door with its forbidding signs. She pushed the door open a crack. She gasped. Tina wasn't in her bed, either.

Angela began running through the apartment. As she ran, she noticed there were no longer any dust balls on the floors. The tabletops had been cleared off and smelled of lemon oil. The laundry which had been piling up while her parents worked on income tax wasn't there. In fact, the whole laundry cart was gone!

The apartment had gotten into a mess in the past week, but now it was clean. Clean and empty.

The kitchen was so clean, it was dazzling. The floor was waxed and the counters looked so white and shiny, the kitchen looked brand new — like an advertisement in a magazine.

Angela held her breath, and went to the refrigerator and opened the door.

There was nothing in the refrigerator.

Angela's heart was pounding. It suddenly hit her. Her family hadn't run away. They had been taken away. They had been taken away by the

Internal Revenue Service because they had failed to get their taxes in.

Angela stood in the front hall wondering what would become of her. She tried to think clearly. Maybe she would ask the doorman to take care of her. She could help him sort the mail. She could keep an eye on the people coming in and out. She wouldn't be any trouble.

A key was turning in the lock. Someone was coming into the apartment.

"A new family," she told herself. "New people moving in." The new tenants would not be pleased to see Angela in their new apartment. She looked around for someplace to hide, but her feet did not seem willing to move.

The door opened slowly and the laundry cart came in, loaded with neatly folded clothes and sheets. Angela's father was pushing the cart. He was whistling.

"Good morning, Angela," he said. "I just met your friend Madeline down in the laundry room."

Just at that moment Tina came out of Nathaniel's room covered with green paint.

"Want to help paint the dollhouse roof?" she asked Angela. "I just did the shutters and it looks wonderful." Tina turned to her father. "Happy Income Tax Day," Tina said. "Congratulations."

Angela stared at Tina and then at her father, who was smiling at her.

"Your mom went to get some fresh croissants and the Sunday paper," he told Angela. "We're having a special breakfast to celebrate getting our taxes in. What a night! When we got down to the post office, we found out that when April fifteenth falls on a Saturday, taxes don't have to be mailed until just before midnight of the next business day."

Tina gasped. "You mean, you didn't have to get them in until Monday?"

Her father laughed. "That's right, but we mailed them anyway. That was just the beginning! We found out that the buses stop running after midnight. We hadn't brought enough money for a taxi. Since we were stranded downtown, we decided to go to an all-night diner. By the time we got back, we weren't even sleepy. We had drunk too much coffee. So we thought we'd clean up. . . ."

He stopped and looked at Angela. "Angela," he said. "Is something the matter?"

The Right Type

"I thought everyone had gone and left me," was all Angela would say.

"Why would we do that?" her father asked.

"I just thought," Angela murmured.

A moment later her mother came in carrying a stack of white boxes tied with string.

"I went wild at the bakery," she began, but she took one look at Angela and said, "What's wrong? What happened?"

Tina said, "Angela thought we all went off and left her."

Jessica Steele looked down at her youngest

child. Angela was in her pajamas, staring down at her bare feet.

She knelt down and took Angela in her arms.

"Why in the world would we ever leave *you*?" she whispered.

Angela finally raised her eyes and looked at the faces clustered around her — her mother, her father, Tina — all looking so worried.

Didn't they remember? Didn't they remember the terrible thing she had done?

Well, she certainly wasn't going to remind them.

All morning Angela wondered if her entire family had gone crazy. No one said a word about her crime.

They had a lovely Sunday breakfast at the dining room table. Stuffed full of pastries and croissants, her parents finally felt sleepy enough to go to bed.

They had been up all night. Angela knew that, but she was shocked that they had gone to sleep without even mentioning the 1040 form.

Where was her punishment?

Angela couldn't help feeling a little suspicious. Was there a plot?

Tina seemed to welcome her company as they painted the dollhouse roof dark green. She even told Angela a secret. Tina had decided to become a city planner when she grew up, but Angela wasn't to tell anyone yet.

"Of course," Tina went on, "I would want to be in a kind of partnership. I don't want to work alone. And you know, I was thinking that Doug might be a good business partner . . . not now, of course. I mean way after I finish high school and college. . . ."

Angela listened to Tina and she felt very wise. She had a feeling that Tina liked Doug a lot. She was amazed that Tina didn't even know it herself even though she was six years older than Angela.

Nathaniel was doing his homework at his desk and their parents were still asleep when the telephone rang.

Tina got to her feet. Then she stopped, and turned pale.

"Answer it, Nathaniel," she told her brother. "If it's Melissa, say I'm not here."

"But you are," Nathaniel said.

"I can't talk to her," Tina said. And she looked

so panicky, Nathaniel said, "I'll say you can't come to the phone."

He went to answer it. Tina sighed. "Well, it *is* sort of true. I *am* covered with paint."

Angela noticed that both she and Tina had dark green paint all over their hands and arms. Angela's smock had been covered with white paint from the day before, so she had decided to wear a T-shirt and jeans, just like Tina's.

Nathaniel returned, went back to his desk and sat down. Then he mumbled, "It's for you, Tina."

Tina wailed, "But I told you I can't talk to Melissa!"

"It's not Melissa," Nathaniel said. "I don't know who it is."

"Oh." Tina went to the front hall. But she couldn't pick up the phone with wet paint all over her hands. So she ran to get a rag to hold over the receiver.

"Hello?" Tina said.

"How are you, darling?"

It was Melissa's mother. It was Mrs. Glenn.

"Are you there, Tina?" Mrs. Glenn had a lovely clear voice with a little bit of an English accent even though she had lived in the United States her whole life.

"I'm here," was all Tina could manage to get out. She waited.

"Melissa was hoping you had a chance to ask your parents about Camp Sunset." Mrs. Glenn's voice sounded a little strained. "She said she won't go back unless you go, too. Of course Camp Sunset is a marvelous experience for anyone, but especially for someone like you, Tina."

Tina knew that Mrs. Glenn had been a Sunset girl herself, and had told Tina more than once that Tina would make "the perfect Sunset girl."

"I can't ask my parents right now," Tina burst out. "I'm really sorry. You see, they stayed up all night doing their income tax."

Mrs. Glenn laughed. Her laugh always sounded like the tinkling of bells. "But darling, certainly they didn't try to do their income tax themselves. Don't they have an accountant?"

"I don't think so." Tina was embarrassed to admit that her parents did not have an accountant.

"Well, we have the sweetest little man," Mrs. Glenn said, "and you might mention him to your parents when next April comes around. . . ."

Finally Mrs. Glenn got back to the subject.

"Well, I certainly didn't call you to try to *push* you into going to Camp Sunset — "

"But I want to go," Tina burst out. "I want to go more than anything in the world!"

"Wonderful!" Mrs. Glenn sounded relieved. "Well, as it happens, Mrs. Minne is in town this weekend, you know, the camp director. . . ."

Tina had often heard Melissa talk about Mrs. Minne (she called her "Minne-ha-ha" behind her back) and how much all the girls hated her.

"I spoke to Mrs. Minne last night. I was most distressed to hear there are very few openings at the camp. You know, she only takes a limited number of new campers." Mrs. Glenn sounded very worried. "In any case, I said, 'Tina Steele simply has to be accepted; she is a Sunset girl through and through.' "

"Thank you," Tina said politely.

"But," Mrs. Glenn went on, "Melissa has probably told you what a silly old snob Mrs. Minne is. She likes to meet all the new campers to make sure they are the Right Type."

Tina felt very confused. Up until now, all she

had thought about was how much money it might cost. But now she realized she might not even be accepted!

"Well, Tina dear, I hope you don't mind, but I arranged a little gathering this afternoon for you to meet Mrs. Minne. Melissa's invited a few of her camp friends who live in the area — a sort of mini-reunion."

"But — " Tina said.

"So we'll expect you around four." Mrs. Glenn now sounded more businesslike, as if she were in a hurry to get off the phone, but she added, "Angela, too, since Angela will be ready to be a Sunset girl in a year or two."

"Angela's invited?"

"Of course," Mrs. Glenn said. "In fact, she's called a Little Sunset Sister until the time she is enrolled in the camp."

"How cute." Tina wasn't sure she wanted her little sister at the same camp.

"My dear Tina, I'm afraid I'm going to have to cut this conversation short." Mrs. Glenn's voice had now become quite crisp and distant. "My oven bell just went off and the cake for the party will be burnt if I chat with you a moment longer."

Tina didn't want to ruin Mrs. Glenn's cake. Melissa's mother baked everything from scratch; she never used cake mixes.

"Thank you very much for the invitation," Tina said. "But . . . um . . . what are people going to wear?"

"Oh, it's an informal gathering, but I suppose you should make a little effort to impress dear old Mrs. Minne."

"Should we wear dresses?" Tina asked.

"Well, of course," Mrs. Glenn said. "Tina, I simply have to get off the phone. We'll see you two at four o'clock."

Tina said good-bye and walked back to Nathaniel's room in a daze.

"Angela," Tina said, "we're going to a party at Melissa's house."

"Me?" A look of wonder came over Angela's face. "I'm invited to Melissa's house? To a party?"

Angela couldn't believe her ears. She had never seen the inside of Melissa's house. And yet for the past two years she had walked to school with Tina and Melissa.

Melissa had never taken any interest in Angela.

She treated her like a package that had to be dropped off.

Angela wondered if something fishy was going on. Maybe everyone was being nice to her as a punishment — to punish her for stealing the 1040 form and ruining Income Tax Day.

She could just see it. Getting all ready for the party and then Tina saying, "By the way, Angela, that was a joke. You're not really invited to the party. Mom and Dad are waiting to punish you instead."

Angela had a scary thought: What if there wasn't going to be a punishment? And — if there was no punishment — how could Angela be forgiven?

I could say "I'm sorry," she thought.

But then, she would be reminding them of her terrible deed.

At two o'clock that afternoon, Tina and Angela finished painting the roof of the dollhouse.

"We're getting dressed for the party starting now," Tina told Angela. "We have to look exactly right. You're going to wear that rose-colored corduroy jumper and a nice blouse, white tights, party shoes. . . . And I'm going to wear . . ."

But first they had to get the paint off.

Tina took Angela to the bathroom sink, and, to her distress, quickly found out that the green paint they had been using was not a water-based paint. Scrubbing with soap and water only spread the paint until their hands and arms were a dull shade of light green — "monster-green," Tina muttered. They were also very sticky.

"Nathaniel," Tina called. "Please get the turpentine. And hurry!"

Nathaniel called back. "I'm doing my homework. You get it."

"I can't," Tina said.

"Tell Angela to get it."

"She can't," Tina called from the bathroom. "We're both covered with paint."

"Well, all right," Nathaniel grumbled.

Nathaniel took a very long time to come back. He finally knocked on the bathroom door and said, "There isn't any. We must have run out yesterday."

Tina and Angela looked at each other. Then they looked down at their arms and hands.

"Oh, please, Nathaniel," Tina begged through the bathroom door. "Please go to the hardware store and get us some. We need it — it's an emergency!"

"Can't," Nathaniel said. "It's not open. Today's Sunday."

Tina looked at her watch. It was already three o'clock. It would take ten minutes to walk to Melissa's house . . . maybe fifteen with Angela. They had to be prompt. She had a feeling that Minne-ha-ha would be displeased if they arrived late.

She made a decision fast.

"Listen, Angela," she said. "Go and put on your blouse with long sleeves, your pink jumper, white tights and black party shoes . . . right now!"

"But, I'll get paint all over my clothes," Angela pointed out.

Tina thought about that. Not only were their hands very sticky, but paint was still coming off — all over the sink.

"Right," Tina said. "Go get the little white gloves Grandma sent you and put them on first. . . . I'll do the same thing."

"They'll be all sticky," Angela said. "Inside. We won't be able to get them off."

"We can worry about that later," Tina said. "In fact, I've got it! We'll just keep them on. We'll wear them to the party. Minne-ha-ha will approve of white gloves. She'll think we're definitely the Right Type!"

Tina made Nathaniel fetch the gloves and put them on both her hands and Angela's. "Like two surgeons in the operating room," Nathaniel said, grinning at them.

Then, with their gloves on, they both went to their rooms to get dressed. No paint got on their clothes.

Tina brushed her hair and looked in the mirror when she was finished. She had picked out a long-sleeved blouse (her arms were still green underneath), and her black velvet jumper, white tights and flat black pumps.

Very proper, she thought. The white gloves really do help.

Tina met Angela in the front hall, looking very sweet in her rose-colored jumper, white shirt, white tights and party shoes.

"But the gloves feel funny," she said to Tina.

Tina understood. Her gloves also felt sticky. It was quite uncomfortable.

"Just try to keep your mind off your hands," Tina said briskly. It was twenty minutes to four. "We've got to leave right now. Nathaniel said he would tell Mom and Dad when they wake up."

Just then she noticed a big patch of green paint in Angela's curly dark hair.

"Oh, no!" Tina was horrified. "You can't go like that. We have to get it out. But how are we going to wash it out with gloves on? We'll get them wet."

"I'll get it out," Angela said. "Don't worry, Tina. I know a way. I'll be right back."

Angela disappeared and came back a minute later, looking quite proud of herself. There was no green paint in her hair.

There was a bald spot instead.

"I cut it out," Angela said proudly. "How does my hair look now?"

Tina's heart sank. Angela looked like a child with a terrible disease. "We're putting your hair in bunches," she told Angela. "Right this minute."

"But bunches are babyish," Angela protested.

"Bunches," Tina said firmly, and very shortly Angela had two cute bunches with pink velvet ribbons on each. One of the bunches had been placed carefully to conceal the bald spot. . . .

As they were putting on their coats, their mother came into the hall. She had just woken up. Nathaniel had told her about Melissa's party, but Tina had not even told Nathaniel it had anything to do with Camp Sunset.

Jessica Steele smiled at her two girls with pleasure. "Don't you both look lovely. And those white gloves! How nice. I didn't know children wore gloves anymore. Grandma will be delighted when I tell her. Well, have fun!"

A Bowl of Cherries

Angela skipped along next to Tina on the way to Melissa's house. She listened as Tina explained the purpose of the party.

"Mrs. Glenn invited me?" Angela asked. At last she believed she was truly invited to Melissa Glenn's house. It wasn't a trick.

"Oh, Tina!" Angela took her sister's hand — something she hadn't done for months. (She was, after all, a first-grader.) "Am I going to get to see Melissa's bed?"

For years she had heard about Melissa's perfect room — her enormous bed with a pink organdy canopy over it, a pink bedspread, and the window seat covered with pink-ruffled cushions.

"And Tina! Tina! Tina! Will I get to see Mrs. Glenn's closet?"

Angela had heard tales of the enormous wardrobe closet filled with outfits for every occasion — just like a doll's wardrobe!

Suddenly Tina stopped and grabbed Angela's arm.

"Angela, I can't promise you anything," she said. "We have to play it by ear. But the most important thing is not to act impressed about anything. Not if you want to be a Little Sunset Sister. The Right Type."

"What does *impressed* mean?" Angela asked.

"You just act like you've seen all those things before," Tina explained.

"But I've never even been inside a house!" Angela said. "I've only seen the inside of houses on television and pictures of them in books."

It was true. Angela was a city child. Everyone she had ever visited lived in apartment houses. Even her grandmother and her Aunt Patty who lived in small towns very far away lived in apartments.

"It will be my first house," Angela said dreamily.

Tina tightened her grip on Angela's arm. "Well, whatever you say, don't say *that!*"

As they walked the rest of the way, Tina gave Angela a quick lesson in etiquette.

" 'Please' and 'thank you,' of course, and always say the grown-up's last name when you answer them — for instance, 'Thank you, *Mrs. Glenn.*' " Tina checked her watch and walked faster. ". . . the same with Minne-ha-ha. . . ."

As they walked up the front path to Melissa's house, Tina added, "Remember, whatever you do, don't act impressed."

"White gloves?" Mrs. Glenn asked when she opened the door. "How lovely! Why, we had to wear them all the time when I was a girl, but we had to wear hats, too. Melissa absolutely refuses to wear gloves."

"Charming," murmured the camp director, a ruddy-faced woman with white hair. She was wearing a tweed suit and sensible shoes. Her blue eyes crinkled up at the corners. Her mouth smiled. But the rest of her face didn't move. Angela felt a little frightened.

Melissa came running down the stairs.

"Stairs!" Angela thought, staring at her first real staircase. But then she remembered she had to pretend she had seen millions of staircases before.

"Oh, it's just another old staircase," she told herself in a strict voice.

Melissa stopped and stared at Tina's white gloves. "Are you serious, Tina? Take those gloves off right now. Everyone's upstairs. Come on."

Tina followed Melissa up the stairs, but she did not take off the gloves.

Angela was standing in the front hall with Mrs. Glenn and the camp director Tina had called Minnie Haha.

"*Mrs.* Haha, to *me!*" Angela reminded herself.

"Angela, darling," Mrs. Glenn said. "Come into the sun parlor. Come meet another lovely Little Sunset Sister. Her name is Muffy."

"Yes, please, Mrs. Glenn," Angela said.

She allowed Melissa's housekeeper to take her coat and followed Mrs. Glenn past a large oil painting in the front hall. For years Angela had heard about this painting. It was a painting of Melissa when she was young, with a watering can.

Mrs. Glenn was talking about it to Mrs. Haha. "Well, I suppose it's worth a fortune today. The artist has become extremely well known. Perhaps you have heard of . . ."

Angela did not even dare look up at the portrait as they passed it. She was afraid she might look impressed. It was a pity. She had waited so long to see it.

Tina felt slightly overwhelmed. There were only three of Melissa's camp friends in the bedroom, but they surrounded her as she sat on Melissa's pink canopy bed and filled her in on all sorts of things about Camp Sunset.

Every once in a while, Melissa glared at Tina and said, "You still have your gloves on, Tina."

"I have to," Tina told her.

"Why?" Melissa insisted.

"I don't want to talk about it," Tina said.

"My mother once made me wear white gloves," a girl with long, white-blonde hair told Tina. "It was this concert. . . ."

Tina tried to relax and enjoy herself.

In a half hour they were to go down to the parlor

to see slides of Camp Sunset and hear Mrs. Minne give her "pitch," as Melissa called it.

"What a witch Minne-ha-ha is," the girl with white-blond hair was saying. "Remember the time she caught us . . . ?"

Tina felt a little better. They were all enjoying telling camp stories, but she had a feeling it was for her benefit!

I think they like me, she thought happily. Maybe I *am* a Sunset girl.

Angela spread the skirt of her pink corduroy jumper carefully around her on the white couch in the room Mrs. Glenn called the sun parlor. Everything was white except for the glass tables and the plants growing in the windows all around the room.

Muffy, the other Little Sunset Sister, had apparently not noticed Angela yet. Mrs. Haha had introduced them, but Muffy obviously hadn't heard the introduction. She was wearing a blue sailor dress and sat curled up next to her baby-sitter.

The baby-sitter said "hello" to Angela. Then

Mrs. Glenn told Angela that was all the English she knew; she spoke only French. Angela felt sorry for her. Her name was Babette and Mrs. Glenn told Angela that Babette was Muffy's "O Pear" girl.

It made sense to Angela. Babette was shaped like a pear. She had wide hips and a very narrow head. She was quiet and very pretty with long, straight, dark hair and green eyes. She spoke only French with Mrs. Glenn. Angela figured Muffy must speak French, too.

So it didn't matter so much that Muffy hadn't noticed Angela, or heard her say "hello." They wouldn't be able to talk to each other anyway.

All the big campers were upstairs in Melissa's bedroom. Tina was up there, too. Mrs. Glenn was sitting with Mrs. Haha having a nice long talk.

"Muffy might even be blind, too," Angela told herself. Muffy was staring right through her now. Angela smiled, but Muffy turned sharply away and looked up at Babette.

In the middle of the glass table in front of the couch was a big bowl of Bing cherries.

"How in the world did you ever find Bing

cherries in the middle of April?" Mrs. Haha asked Mrs. Glenn. "I didn't think it was possible."

"Well, I understand from my fruit vendor there's a little man in Chile who actually raises them!"

"How marvelous!" Mrs. Haha said.

Mrs. Glenn gave Angela a smile. "Angela, don't you want to try one?"

Angela shook her head. Her gloves were stuck to her hands, and she did not want to get cherry juice on them.

"Sweetheart," Mrs. Glenn said, "you could take off your gloves now."

"I can't . . . I mean, I'm not allowed to," Angela said. Not only were the gloves stuck to her hands — for the rest of her life perhaps — but her hands itched terribly. "I mean, I'm not allowed to, *Mrs. Glenn.*"

Mrs. Glenn laughed and turned to Mrs. Haha. "I never ever contradict another child's parents."

But the cherries looked beautiful. They were in a glass bowl that Mrs. Glenn had already explained to the camp director "was priceless — wedding crystal. If it broke, I don't know what I would do."

Angela didn't want to get too close to that bowl.

Babette suddenly reached over and picked up the bowl. She offered Angela a cherry.

Angela didn't want to hurt Babette's feelings so she carefully took a cherry. She held it very delicately. She did not want to squeeze it.

She put it in her mouth and ate it. It was delicious. But of course, she still had the pit in her mouth. She looked all over the table. Where in the world was she supposed to put the pit?

Babette offered Angela another cherry and then another. Angela had a mouth full of pits, but no place to put them. Angela was the only one in the room eating cherries, and Tina had not included cherry pits in her speed course in etiquette.

Finally her mouth was so full, she simply took the pits out and held them tightly in her fist so no one could see all the red stains on her white glove. If the stains didn't come out, Angela was sure her grandmother would understand, especially if her gloves never came off, either.

Tina was beginning to feel quite comfortable. The girl with the white-blonde hair was named Lila and she was very funny. She sat cross-legged on the floor, even though she was wearing a dress.

Lila seemed to think Tina was an excellent audience, and Tina wondered if, some day, they might be best friends.

Lila swung her hair back, pushed her fingers through it and went on with the story.

"So anyway, this girl in our cabin, Joan. . . ."

Everyone groaned at the name Joan.

"We hated her. I mean, we couldn't *stand* her. So it's her birthday, right? But we pretend not to know. We don't say a word all morning and she gets this tragic expression on her face. . . ."

Tina tried not to feel sorry for Joan.

"She comes back to the cabin after lunch and we're all behind the door and jump out. 'Surprise!' we scream. Joan nearly has a heart attack, but she's finally happy. Silly smile on her face — the whole thing. We give her a present, right? She opens it. And it's a blouse . . . cute . . . baby doll sleeves . . . little bumblebees all over it. . . . She goes to try it on and guess what!"

Tina said, "What?" but she wasn't enjoying this story as much as the others Lila had told.

"There's a real bumblebee inside the blouse.

She gets this bee sting right here. . . ." Lila pointed to her waist.

Tina felt sick. She looked around. Melissa, Stephanie, and the other girl whose name was Chickie were rolling around the floor laughing.

Lila kept going. "Pain all day. She's crying. Wants to go home. Parents take her out of camp. They lose a couple of grand. . . ."

"A couple of grand?" Tina asked. She knew Lila was talking about money. She always had trouble remembering if *grand* meant a hundred dollars or a thousand.

"Right," Lila said. "They lost the whole camp fee for the summer."

Tina didn't feel like laughing or even smiling. She just hoped she would be able to get through the slide show.

Angela sat clutching the cherry pits and tried to pay attention to the slide show. Tina sat surrounded by a bunch of girls on the other white couch, but she didn't look as if she were having a very good time.

The slide show wasn't so interesting even

though Angela thought the lake and sunset pictures were kind of pretty.

" . . . back to nature . . . the simple outdoor life. . . ."

Mrs. Haha wasn't so interesting, either, and Angela saw the girls give each other looks behind the camp director's back. Angela felt a little sorry for her.

To Angela's surprise, Muffy suddenly started speaking English as soon as her sister Lila came downstairs. Angela felt a little hurt. Muffy had been ignoring her!

They all had some cake, but Angela refused the plate Mrs. Glenn offered her. "No, thank you, Mrs. Glenn."

She knew she couldn't eat with her left hand and her right hand was all tied up with cherry pits.

Suddenly Tina stood up and said, "Angela and I have to leave now. Thank you very much, Mrs. Glenn."

Tina turned to the camp director and shook her hand. "We promised to be home by six," she said. "It was nice to meet you."

"It will be a pleasure to have you at camp this summer," the camp director said.

Angela sat up straight. She was horrified. Her sister had forgotten to use the camp director's last name!

Angela looked around to see if anyone was watching and then quickly tucked the cherry pits under a white cushion.

She stood up. Tina had gone to get her coat. Angela knew she had to make up for her sister's rudeness.

She couldn't shake hands the way Tina did — not with all that red juice on her hands — so she curtsied to Mrs. Glenn. "Thank you very much for the party, Mrs. Glenn."

Mrs. Glenn ruffled her hair. "Isn't she adorable?" she asked the camp director. "Why, I haven't seen a curtsy in years."

"A peach." The camp director smiled her scary smile. "We look forward to seeing you in a couple of years," she told Angela.

Angela curtsied again. "Nice to meet you, Mrs. Haha," she said and skipped out of the room.

Tina was already at the front door waiting for

Angela. She looked very confused. She was in a hurry.

On the way home Angela suddenly remembered the cherry pits. Her heart sank. Sooner or later Mrs. Glenn would find them — or the housekeeper would.

Angela looked sadly up at her sister. She couldn't tell Tina that she had just ruined everything. Tina would never be a Sunset girl!

Vacation Plans

Tina took Angela's hand and walked home very fast. Her hands felt stiff and itchy. She wanted to throw up every time she thought of the poor bumblebee trapped in Joan's blouse. She felt sorry for Joan, too. What a birthday present!

The cruelty of the trick made her sick to her stomach. Tina knew the bee must have died soon after it stung Joan.

Tina wanted to throw up in the privacy of her own bathroom, not on the street. She hurried and Angela hurried along beside her.

Her mother opened the door, and Tina didn't feel quite so nauseous.

"What happened?" her mother said, looking from Tina to Angela.

"It doesn't matter," Tina said. "The first thing we have to do is get these gloves off. Then I'll throw up."

"I don't understand." Her mother looked very confused.

"Mom!" Tina wailed. "Can't you see? They're stuck to our hands! We only put them on because we couldn't get the paint off."

"Our hands are all green," Angela explained. "So are our arms."

"Didn't you use a water-base paint?" Tina's mother asked.

Tina said, "No, the green enamel. We're out of turpentine." She was feeling a little better.

Her mother didn't ask any more questions. She went next door and borrowed a cup of turpentine from their neighbor.

In no time at all Angela and Tina were soaking their gloved hands in a pan full of water mixed with turpentine. The pan was sitting on the kitchen table.

Nathaniel and Doug walked into the kitchen to see what was going on.

"Hi, Tina. Hi, Angela," Doug said. "The dollhouse looks great."

Tina felt foolish soaking her hands in a pan. She was still all dressed up in her velvet jumper. She mumbled, "Thanks."

The telephone rang. Tina pulled her hands out of the pan.

"Tina! Don't answer it," Angela gasped. "It's going to be Mrs. Glenn. She found them!"

"Found what?" Tina asked.

"I'll get the phone!" their mother called from the living room.

Angela told Tina about the cherry pits under the cushion.

Tina groaned. "Come on, Angela. That's the least of our worries."

"Please don't be Mrs. Glenn," Angela prayed.

Her mother came into the kitchen.

"It's Mrs. Glenn, Tina. Shall I tell her that you'll call her back?"

"No," Tina said. "I'd better talk to her. I think I can get these gloves off now."

"Wait, Tina," her mother said. But Tina peeled off the gloves in a hurry. Her hands were raw and chapped. Her mother gave her a towel to dry them.

"Can I take my hands out of the turpentine, too?" Angela asked her mother.

"Wait a minute, Angela." Mrs. Steele was looking for the cocoa butter.

"Tina, put this on before you answer the telephone."

Tina rubbed the cocoa butter on her hands and went to the hall table. She took a deep breath and picked up the phone.

"Hello, Mrs. Glenn," Tina said.

"Tina, darling, I can't understand why you and Angela left the party in such a hurry." Mrs. Glenn sounded distressed. "The girls were so disappointed. Of course they were immensely amused at Angela's little mistake."

"Huh?" Tina asked. "What mistake?"

"When Angela, poor darling, called her Mrs. Haha. But don't worry about it. Even Mrs. Minne found it amusing. And it's perfectly understandable how the poor dear . . ." Tina was waiting for Mrs. Glenn to get to the point.

"Please tell Angela that Muffy kept asking why she left. . . ."

Melissa's mother went on and on about what a

hit Tina and Angela had made at the party. Finally she said:

"But the important thing is that Mrs. Minne wanted to give you a few brochures for your parents and the application, of course. There aren't many openings at this late date."

Tina was quiet a moment. She wanted to be polite.

"Mrs. Glenn," she said, "I don't think I'll be going to Camp Sunset after all, but thank you anyway."

There was a silence. "I don't understand," Mrs. Glenn said sharply. "Was someone mean to you? Those girls can be a little rude."

"No," Tina said. "The party was lovely, but I have other plans for the summer."

"Well, why didn't you say something before I went to all that trouble?" Mrs. Glenn asked.

"I didn't know about these plans until I got home," Tina lied. "But to be honest, I guess I'm not the Sunset type."

"I *knew* those girls had said something. I *told* Melissa. . . . Tina, please. . . ."

"I have to get off the phone now," Tina said. "I'm really sorry, Mrs. Glenn."

"Melissa will be heartbroken," Mrs. Glenn said.

"Tell her I'll talk to her tomorrow." Tina wanted to get out of her party dress.

Mrs. Glenn finally let her go.

Tina went back to the kitchen. Doug and Nathaniel were having a snack at the table. Angela still had her hands in the turpentine. Her face was bright red.

Angela said, "Did she find the cherry pits?"

"No," Tina said. "She wasn't exactly calling about cherry pits."

"Did you tell her about them?"

"No." Tina sat down at the kitchen table with Nathaniel and Doug. "I have nothing to do this summer," she said dully.

"Well, why didn't you tell her?" Angela asked.

Tina looked thoughtfully at Angela. Angela almost never cried but her eyes were very bright.

"Now she's going to find them and know who it is," Angela said. "She'll think I tried to hide them."

"Well, you did," Tina said. "Oh honestly, Angela, there are some things more important than

Mrs. Glenn's white slipcovers. Don't you understand? I'm not going to Camp Sunset. I don't even want to go. But now I don't have anything to do this summer."

"Look, Tina," Doug said. "I'm trying to get Nathaniel a job as a junior counselor at the camp I work at. Maybe you could work there, too. You're old enough to be a counselor-in-training. It's a great camp."

Tina turned to Nathaniel. "Did you ask Mom and Dad?" she asked.

"Not yet. I don't even know if I got the job," Nathaniel said. "I filled out an application, but I haven't heard from Reverend Jones yet."

"He's the camp director," Doug told Tina.

"Tina, Tina, Tina, could you call her back?" Angela begged. "Could you *please* call her back?"

"Cherry pits are not the most important thing right now, Angela," Tina said. She turned to Doug. "Do you really think . . . ?"

Angela peeled off her gloves very quickly, dried her hands and rubbed the cocoa butter into them. Then she left the kitchen.

"What's wrong with Angela?" Nathaniel asked.

"I don't know," Tina said. "I don't know why

she's taking those cherry pits so seriously."

"What are you talking about?" Nathaniel asked.

When Tina described the scene in the sun parlor, Nathaniel and Doug laughed.

"I'll bet that camp costs a fortune," Nathaniel said.

"But they don't even have electricity in the cabins," Tina said. "It's very simple, back to nature — "

"Oh, come on, Tina," Nathaniel said. "You told me Melissa's friends from camp were a bunch of snobs. The camp is probably just saving money on electricity. I'll bet Melissa's parents pay a couple of grand each summer."

"What does *grand* mean?" Tina asked. "Is it a hundred dollars or a thousand?"

"A thousand," Doug said. "Why?"

"I just wondered," Tina said.

Angela sat with her parents in the living room after dinner. Tina and Nathaniel had gone to Doug's house. Doug's mother had called Reverend Jones, who apologized for being so slow in answering Nathaniel's application for the camp job. Nathaniel had the job! Not only that — Tina was badly needed as a counselor-in-training. She wouldn't get paid, of course, but. . . .

Angela felt miserable. She kept thinking about the cherry pits. And, when she wasn't thinking about the cherry pits, she was thinking about how she ruined Income Tax Day.

She sat in her little rocking chair, waiting for Mrs. Glenn to call back with the terrible discovery.

Her father was snoozing on the couch and listening to music. Her mother was reading a mystery story.

The telephone rang and Angela felt cold all over. She was sure it was Mrs. Glenn.

But it wasn't Mrs. Glenn. It was Angela's Aunt Patty. Her mother's sister called long distance every Sunday night.

"Guess what, Patty," Angela heard her mother say. "It looks like Tina and Nathaniel will be working at a camp this summer."

Angela wanted to go to the camp, too, but no one had mentioned anything to her.

Her mother went on. "Well, you know, I think it will be good for them and for us, too. They have been doing an awful lot of fighting lately. I can't say I mind getting them out of the house."

Angela sat up straight. She was shocked to hear her mother talk that way.

"... but we haven't had a vacation in years," her mother was saying, "and we did a little better this year than we thought we would. We were thinking of a few weeks in Maine — at that fishing camp in the Rangeley Lakes — the one we went to on our honeymoon."

Angela pricked up her ears. She knew she was "eavesdrooping" or whatever it was called, but she had to hear what her mother was saying.

"Wouldn't it be lovely?" Her mother sounded so happy. "I haven't seen trees and forests in so long. Richard and I haven't had time to ourselves in years. . . ." She paused and listened to something Aunt Patty said.

"Angela?" her mother said. "Oh my goodness! I forgot all about Angela!"

Bedtime Story

Angela was not surprised to have been forgotten. That was probably the reason why they had never punished her for taking the 1040 form. Her parents had simply forgotten there *was* an Angela.

Angela stood up, gave her snoring father a little kiss on the cheek and went to her room.

She sat down at the worktable, took out the stationery her grandmother had sent to her and settled down to write to Flor Elena.

Flor Elena wrote to the Steele family once a month, but Angela wrote to Flor Elena once a week.

Angela took out the letter the Steele family had received over a year ago from the nurse who had discovered Flor Elena on the verge of starvation. Tina had read the letter to Angela many times and she knew every word in it by heart:

Dear Mr. and Mrs. Steele, Tina, Nathaniel and Angela:

Flor Elena was only six years old when I saw her sitting on the dusty city sidewalk chewing on a gasoline-soaked rag. She was chewing on the rag so she would not feel the pain of hunger. There were older children around — the street beggars — but no one knew who she was or where she had come from. And she was too weak to talk about her past.

With your kind check of $17, we fed Flor Elena and also tried to trace her family. After some research, we learned that her family had been wiped out by the drought to the northwest of this city.

But we located her mother's best friend, Elena, a young widow, who works for our Forest Service. Flor Elena now lives with her on a remote peninsula in the southwest and has plenty to eat.

With the same money we bought her her first little book. (She had never seen a book before and held it upside down at first.)

We were pleased to see how quickly she recovered. Her schoolwork is done by mail, and her foster mother is helping her learn English. She seems a bright and happy child.

By some miracle, it seems, she has not suffered the permanent brain and bodily damage so often caused by severe malnutrition.

> *Bless your hearts,*
> *Maria Sanchez, R. N.*

Angela knew that Flor Elena was now seven years old. At first she had been quite disappointed that the orphan she had helped rescue was older than she was. She had hoped for an orphan baby.

Flor Elena's letters were short and to the point. She asked after the Steele family's health. Then she wrote about her sheep and her chickens who had died in the drought and how she missed them.

She always ended by thanking the family, once again, for being her friend.

Angela often dreamed about visiting Flor Elena. "She must live in a beautiful country," Angela thought. The stamps on her envelopes were lovely: birds, flowers and wild animals. . . .

Dear Flor Elena, (Angela began)

How are you? I am fine.
Yesterday was Income Tax Day and today I went to a party with Tina at Melissa's house.

When are you coming to visit? I hope it will be soon.

Your Friend,
Angela Steele

Angela wanted to write more, but she couldn't

tell Flor Elena about the problem the United States was having with the national debt. She didn't want to worry Flor Elena, who lived in another country.

Angela felt sad. She was sad because she was sure Flor Elena was *not* going to visit soon. She was still too poor.

Angela got ready for bed. Her mother brought her the envelope, all addressed, for Flor Elena, as she did every Sunday night.

She kissed Angela and tucked her in. "What happened to your hair?" she asked.

Angela had forgotten about the bald spot on her head.

"Cutting out paint," Angela murmured.

"Oh, Angela." Her mother sighed, and gave her another kiss. "Isn't it wonderful about Tina's and Nathaniel's jobs for the summer?"

Angela pretended not to hear.

"Would you like a story tonight?"

Angela nodded.

"What story do you want me to read?" she asked.

Angela climbed out of bed and went to her bookcase. She reached for the book of fairy tales. Then she changed her mind.

"No story," she said. "I want to read to myself."

"How nice," her mother said. "You can leave the light on for fifteen minutes."

"Good night, Mommy," Angela said. "Please close my door."

As soon as her mother had gone, Angela went to her bookcase and took out *Hansel and Gretel*.

She snuggled up under her covers and began to read:

Once there was a little boy
and a little girl.
The boy's name was Hansel and
the girl's name was Gretel.
They lived with their father
and their stepmother
near a big forest. . . .
But times were bad.
People did not have enough money . . .

Angela felt peaceful reading a nice familiar tale. And now that she was a first-grader, she could pick out a lot of the words. She already knew the whole story by heart. Her family had taken turns reading it to her when she was younger.

"*I know what to do,*" *his wife said.*
"*Early tomorrow morning,*
we will take the children deep into the
forest and leave them there. . . ."

Angela always pretended that she was Gretel and Eddie Bishop, her reading partner, was Hansel.

"*Don't cry, little sister,*" *Hansel said.*
"*We will find our way home*
as soon as the moon comes up."

Angela whispered the story to herself.

When she got to the part where Gretel saves Hansel, she made sure that Gretel remembered to put on oven mitts before she pushed the wicked old witch into the oven.

Angela changed the end of the story, too. With the diamonds and pearls they found hidden in the witch's house, they bought real shampoo for Hansel, and spent the rest of the money on a mansion for Eddie's grandmother and a plane ticket to the United States for Flor Elena.

"*. . . and* when they got back to the woodcutter's

cottage, they found still another wicked old witch who ate children living there. . . ."

So Hansel and Gretel's misfortunes and adventures could go on and on.

Angela turned off the light and closed her eyes. She thought about the stuffed elephant she had had when she was younger. She thought about Flor Elena. Finally she went to sleep.

Other Arrangements

On Monday morning Angela waited for Tina in the front hall and hoped they would not be late for school. (Tina was wetting her hair so that she could blow it dry all over again.)

There was a photograph album lying open on the hall table. Angela looked at the photographs. She had never seen them before.

They were photographs of her mother and father looking very young and happy — her father swimming in a lake, her mother cooking over a campfire in the forest. . . .

"Daddy and I were looking at our honeymoon

photographs last night," her mother told her when she saw Angela looking at the album.

"Oh, let me see!" Tina had come into the hall and she began flipping through the album.

"Oh, Mom!" Tina breathed. "You were so beautiful."

Angela stared at the strange photographs. There was one of her father, looking tanned and healthy. He was standing on a boat dock holding up a big fish.

Angela studied the fish. Its eyes were open, but . . .

Angela gasped. "Is that fish dead?" she asked.

Tina giggled. "Of course it's dead, Angela."

"Daddy won a prize for that fish," her mother said proudly.

Angela thought about the fish she had seen at the fish store — the fish lying in ice, their eyes wide open — the fish she had always assumed died a natural death. "Old age, probably," she told herself.

"Did Daddy catch that fish on purpose?" she asked.

Her mother was puzzled. "Well, of course." She pointed to a picture of a log cabin surrounded by trees. "That's where we stayed." She sighed. "The Bluebird Cabins. And, guess what!"

"What?" Tina asked.

"I called last night and the Bluebird Cabins are still there! The new owners said they also own a more modern camp across the lake, but Daddy and I decided we'd rather stay at the Bluebird Cabins — away from the crowds. I made a reservation for the last week in July and the first week in August, while you and Nathaniel are still away. I thought we'd rent a car. . . ."

Angela was very confused. Where did she fit in?

". . . Angela can have swimming lessons . . ." her mother went on.

Angela was shocked. "I'm not going to Maine!"

"Of course you are," her mother said.

"No," Angela said. "You and Daddy can go."

"Don't be silly," her mother said and she gave Angela a big hug. "You will love it there."

"I can't go," Angela mumbled. "I have to help Madeline feed Moxie the cat."

Her mother laughed. "I'm sure Madeline can make other arrangements. It's only for two weeks."

Just then Angela realized her mother was only including her on the trip so that she wouldn't feel left out. She was sure her parents didn't want her tagging along.

"That's okay," she assured her mother in her most grown-up voice. "You and Daddy can go to Maine, and *I'll* get other arrangements."

"Huh?" Her mother burst out laughing. "What kind of arrangements?"

"I guess I'll just go to camp with Tina and Nathaniel," Angela murmured.

"No you won't," Tina said sharply. "They don't take any campers under eight years old." Tina turned a page in the album and screeched. "Oh, Mom, what a terrific outfit!"

Angela peeked at the photograph of her mother dressed in blue-and-white-striped overalls. She was sitting on a rock on the side of the mountain holding onto a big sun hat with one hand and blowing a kiss to the camera with the other.

"Is Daddy taking that picture?" Angela asked.

"Of course," Tina said. "Isn't it cute?"

Angela did not think it was the least bit cute. There were other people in the photograph — a group of mountain climbers off to the side. All they would have to do is turn around and they would be able to see Angela's mother blowing her father that kiss.

Angela was completely disgusted with her parents. If they thought it was fun to live in a broken-down old cabin, blow kisses in public places and murder fish for the fun of it, that was their problem. Angela would have nothing to do with it.

"I'll make other arrangements," she told herself. She liked the way that sounded.

Melissa Glenn was waiting for Tina and Angela at the corner. Angela wondered what it would be like to stay at Melissa's house while her parents went to Maine. Then she remembered the cherry pits.

Melissa did not say hello. She said, "Angela, you can tell your sister that I'm never speaking to her again unless she goes to Camp Sunset."

Angela looked up at Tina, who tossed her head and said, "Tell Melissa that I couldn't care less."

Melissa and Tina walked Angela to school in stony silence. Angela had to run to keep up with them.

"Cross out Melissa's house," she told herself.

*   *   *

The days were getting warmer and the trees were beginning to bloom. For the next few weeks Angela kept an eye out for places she could stay while her parents went to Maine. She was afraid it would be too expensive for them to send her to her grandmother's or to her Aunt Patty's. They lived very far away.

Right after spring vacation, she had a play date with Mandy, a girl in her first-grade class. She was very impressed with Mandy's toys and the little couch in her room that pulled out into a bed, "for my guests," Mandy told her. But when Mandy's mother yelled at Mandy for breaking her crayons, Angela said to herself, "Cross off Mandy."

On a Monday morning in the middle of May, Angela sat in her classroom thinking over the possibilities.

All during silent reading, she kept peeking up at her teacher.

Miss Mason did not have children of her own; Angela knew that, but that was all she knew about Miss Mason.

Angela wondered if Miss Mason had plans for the summer. "She must get pretty lonely for children when school is over," Angela told herself.

Miss Mason noticed Angela looking at her and smiled. Angela smiled back and looked down again at her book.

There was no doubt in her mind. Miss Mason was her first choice. Certainly her mother and father would be delighted to have her stay with her teacher. Teachers were experts on children.

Angela looked around at her classmates. She thought how jealous they would be if she stayed with Miss Mason.

Just then Angela noticed that Cheryl White was reading and holding her nose at the same time. Cheryl sat next to Angela, and Eddie Bishop sat right behind Cheryl.

Eddie's hair *did* smell cleaner than usual.

"Stop it, Cheryl," Angela whispered, but Cheryl just giggled and fanned her nose.

Eddie looked up and saw what Cheryl was doing. He gave Angela a puzzled look. A moment later Angela saw Eddie checking the bottom of his shoes to see if he had stepped in anything.

When Eddie was called on to read out loud, he missed every word. Cheryl rolled her eyes, sighed and groaned loudly. She spent the entire lunch period telling everyone that Eddie Bishop was "holding the class back."

"He's going to have to repeat first grade," Cheryl said. "He can't read and he can't write."

Angela looked at Eddie. He didn't seem to be listening to Cheryl. He seemed to be thinking about something else.

Angela felt terrible. She was sure it was her fault if Eddie had to repeat first grade. After all, she was Eddie's reading partner.

"Maybe he'll just have to go to summer school," she heard Meredith say to Cheryl. "That's what my cousin did. He went to summer school and didn't have to repeat first grade."

"Don't worry," Cheryl said. "Eddie Bishop will fail summer school, too. Trust me."

Summer school? Angela had never heard of such a thing. It sounded interesting. She figured it was something like summer camp. She pictured little cabins on a lake with teachers instead of counselors.

During the last period of the day, Angela noticed that Eddie didn't even try to answer the questions in the workbook. He just looked out the window.

Every once in a while he stared at Angela with a puzzled expression on his face.

Angela looked at her workbook, which was called *SENTENCE FUN*. The lesson for today was about Susie the Snail, Freddy the Frog and Harry the Hippo. All at once she had an idea.

Very carefully Angela circled all the wrong answers. When she had finished, she went on to the next lesson. She took out a piece of scratch paper. On the scratch paper, she figured out the right answers so that she would be sure to answer every question wrong.

She knew they weren't supposed to work ahead. *SENTENCE FUN* was their last workbook for the year. It was to last them until the end of June.

But Angela figured the faster she worked, the faster she would get left back.

It only seemed fair. If Eddie got left back, Angela would get left back, too. They could go to summer school together, and Angela would not have to go to Maine.

Sentence Fun

Angela was finding it quite interesting to get everything wrong. She had to work double. She had to know the right answer to get the wrong one. She even made sure she fell for the tricks she was supposed to fall for.

She looked up at the clock and moved on to the next lesson: *PUT QUESTION MARKS AFTER THE RIGHT SENTENCES.*

It was quite a challenge. Angela had completed six lessons when she felt something brush against her leg. She looked down.

On the floor next to her foot was a folded-up piece of yellow paper.

She picked it up and opened it.

She read it:

why was she holding her nose? Fill in the ahser here

Angela had never gotten a note before. She knew it was naughty to pass notes. She turned around. Eddie was looking at her.

The note was from Eddie!

Angela did not want Miss Mason to catch Eddie passing notes, so she wrote quickly on the line:

Your hair smells funny. Too clean

She leaned across the aisle and placed it on Eddie's desk. Then she went back to work.

But a few minutes later, the yellow piece of paper was back at her feet.

Angela picked it up and opened it.

On the next line Eddie had written a new message:

My Grandma washes my hair with brown soap. But I CAN use my sister's shampu. OK?

Angela turned around and nodded at Eddie. Eddie was grinning at her. She tucked the note into the pocket of her book bag.

She looked at the clock again. Now she was racing against time. She worked right up to the three o'clock bell.

Angela handed in the workbook. She had finished every lesson in it. She had even checked over many of the answers to make sure they were wrong. Miss Mason would correct them tonight and would probably call her mother tomorrow to tell her that Angela was being left back — that she would have to go away to summer school.

Angela sat on the bench waiting for Tina. She felt she had put in a good day's work.

She reached into her book bag and took out the note from Eddie. It amazed her how easy it had been to tell him the truth in a note. And she had suffered over his hair for months!

But something about that note bothered her.

Eddie had written all the words himself. He had read Angela's answer and understood it. He had spelled almost every word right. He had even put question marks in the right places. Angela had suspected that Eddie had been able to read for a long time, but this proved it.

Angela was sure an illegal note did not count. "Only workbooks and tests count," she told herself.

But, just to be sure, Angela tore the note into tiny pieces and put it back into her book bag. She was even afraid to throw it in the litter basket. She didn't want anyone to find it.

Angela did not want to be left back without Eddie. She did not want to go to summer school by herself.

A Visit to the Post Office

The next day — a month after the United States government received the most cheerful income tax form in history — Angela's first grade class received a letter from the postmaster.

Angela held her breath while Miss Mason read it to the class:

> *Dear Miss Mason and her First Grade Class:*
>
> *Thank you for your interest in the United States Postal Service. We look*

*forward to your visit to our main office
on Friday, May 19, at eleven o'clock in
the morning.*

It was signed *Susan Stapleton, Postmaster.*

Cheryl White raised her hand. "If she's a girl, she can't be a postmaster," she told Miss Mason. "She has to be postmistress."

"Well, no," Miss Mason said slowly. "It doesn't matter if you're a man or a woman. It's always postmaster."

Angela raised her hand.

"Yes, Angela?"

"Is that all she wrote?" she asked. "Is that the end of the letter?"

Miss Mason looked surprised "Well, yes. . . ."

Angela breathed a sigh of relief. She hoped the post office never found out she had sent all those quarters through the mail.

Angela loved her mailman, whose name was Felix. He always seemed happy and surprised to see her. Sometimes he even told her ahead of time if there was a letter or package for her. She didn't want Felix to be disappointed in her.

Cheryl's hand was up again. "Miss Mason," she said. "How come we didn't get our workbooks back?"

Miss Mason looked a little uncomfortable. She glanced at Angela. Then she cleared her throat.

"This week," she said, "we will not be using our workbooks. We will be studying the post office."

"She's probably not finished correcting mine," Angela said to herself.

Miss Mason handed out booklets to everyone in the class. Cheryl took one and passed the rest of them over her shoulder to Eddie without turning around. She was holding her nose.

Angela sniffed and sniffed. Eddie's hair smelled just like everyone else's hair this morning. She decided not to say a word to Cheryl. She would let Cheryl look silly holding her nose for no reason!

Angela opened the booklet. It was all about the post office and the history of the United States mail. There were pictures of early stamps and the pony express riders, poems about the mail carriers and a section called Famous American Mail Carriers.

One story was about Benjamin Franklin, the first postmaster in the days of the colonies. The other was about Charles Lindbergh, a famous aviator who flew the mail.

Eddie seemed to find the book very interesting. Angela could see his lips moving as he read about the pony express riders. She was getting nervous. She looked quickly through the booklet. There were no questions and answers. There were no "fill-in-the-blanks."

So it doesn't count, she told herself with a sigh of relief.

Eddie raised his hand and everyone in the class stared at him. Eddie had never raised his hand before.

"Are these books for us to keep?" he asked in his hoarse voice.

"Yes," Miss Mason said. "They are published by the U. S. Postal Service."

"Wow!" Eddie said.

All that day and the next Eddie carried the booklet around with him. At lunchtime on Thursday, he showed Angela what he had written in the book: *This book belongs to Eddie Bishop.*

". . . and I don't even have a bookcase to put it in," he confided to Angela.

"You can make a bookcase," Angela told him.

"Like mine. Just make it out of bricks and boards. . . ."

Eddie was very interested.

That afternoon the class learned a song about the post office. "The mailman, the mailman, the nicest man of all. He wakes you up in the morning before the bugle call. . . ."

"Wouldn't it be nice if we sang it at the post office tomorrow?" Miss Mason asked. "Maybe there's something else we can do, too. Something the whole class can do."

Eddie's hand was up again.

By the end of the afternoon Eddie and Angela had written a post office cheer. It was based on a saying in their booklet: *Neither snow nor rain nor heat nor gloom of night stays these couriers from the swift completion of their appointed rounds.*

Seven children in the class took turns being the speaker while the rest of the class joined in on the chorus.

It went like this:

SPEAKER	REST OF CLASS
Neither wind	NO! (Howl like wind)

Nor rain	NO!
Nor snow	NO!
Nor sleet nor hail	NO!
Neither heat wave	NO!
nor tidal wave	NO!
Nor gloom of night	NO! (Scary voices)

ALL TOGETHER:

stays these couriers from the swift completion of their appointed rounds.

The mail must go through!
HOORAY FOR THE POSTMAN!

Angela was a little worried about the tidal wave. She didn't want anything to happen to her mailman, Felix.

But Eddie had wanted to add all sorts of disasters: volcanoes, hurricanes, tornadoes and even monsters from Japanese movies wrecking the town.

"Too dangerous," Angela kept saying. "I think the mailman should stay home." But she finally had to give in and let Eddie put in the tidal wave as a compromise.

"They changed the words," Cheryl complained

loudly. "Eddie and Angela changed the words."

"That's all right," Miss Mason said. "Those words are over two thousand years old. They were written about the Persian couriers who carried battle messages on horseback. They were written in Greek by a man named Herodotus." Miss Mason smiled. "I think Herodotus would approve," she said.

The post office certainly approved of their cheer.

The next day, the postmaster, Susan Stapleton, asked them to repeat the cheer for every worker at the main post office. She took them to places other classes had never even seen.

Miss Mason's class had the most wonderful time. Everyone loved the machine that canceled the postage stamps and the sorting machine. Angela was amazed to see so many mailmen who were not Felix.

Tears came to her eyes when she heard about the dead letter office, but she cheered up when the postmaster showed them the change-of-address postcard. "Even if you go away for a few weeks, your mail can be forwarded to you."

Angela took a change-of-address postcard so

that her mail could be sent to her at summer school.

Eddie raised his hand. "You can get your mail sent to you after you're dead, too," he said.

Cheryl White groaned and muttered, "Eddie!" but Susan Stapleton said, "That's right!"

"My grandfather died and he still gets mail," Eddie said. "Even some money that someone owed him."

"But he can't open the letters, right?" Chris asked.

"Right," Eddie said.

It was a comforting thought. The postal service all over the world cared about you from the day you were born, for your whole life and even after you were dead.

Angela and her classmates watched in awe as the big mail trucks rolled out. She was bursting with pride that she, too, had an address. She made a vow to help the post office in any way she could.

"Can you become a citizen of the post office?" she asked the postmaster.

The postmaster laughed and said, "Well, no, but what a lovely question."

It was time to leave. The entire class was gathered around the bulletin board. Eddie was reading the FBI WANTED posters out loud.

Angela looked and saw Miss Mason watching Eddie. She had a very odd look on her face.

"Listen to this," Eddie said. "This guy escaped from prison where he was serving a life sentence for murder." He read, " 'Johnson has a mole under right eye, large scar on right side of face . . . he is armed and considered extremely dangerous.' "

"I think I've seen that guy," Chris said. "I think he works at our gas station. . . ."

Chris wanted to sit with Eddie on the bus on the way back to school. He wanted Eddie to help him remember where he had seen that guy Johnson. Angela let Chris have her seat.

"Come sit with me, Angela," Miss Mason said. "I wanted to talk to you. There's something I have been trying to figure out all week."

Angela went and sat next to Miss Mason.

Her teacher whispered, "Perhaps you can explain to me how you did a whole month's work in your workbook in one hour."

"Yes, but I got all the answers wrong." Angela suddenly realized she couldn't say that. "I mean I *think* I got the answers wrong. It was very, very hard," she added in a sad voice. "I guessed and guessed."

Miss Mason burst out laughing. "Angela," she said. "Do you know that it's just about impossible to get every single answer wrong if you guess? Chances are you'll get one right out of every four."

Angela did not understand.

"Angela, you got every answer wrong on purpose, and you got them wrong on purpose very, very fast. Why?"

"I wanted to go to summer school with Eddie Bishop," Angela murmured. "I didn't want him to get left back all by himself."

"No one gets left back in *my* class," Miss Mason said. "And, believe me, if Eddie can read those WANTED posters, he can read anything. This class is going to get some very hard work from me in the next month."

"You know," Angela confessed to Miss Mason. "It was kind of interesting. You see, I had to figure out the right answers first."

"It certainly was interesting to me," Miss Mason said. "I thought you were just trying to show me how dumb these workbooks are. Angela, we're going to throw those workbooks out the window."

Angela waited all afternoon to throw workbooks out the window, but, as it turned out, Miss Mason just meant they weren't going to use them anymore.

Miss Mason asked Angela if it would be all right with her if Eddie corrected her workbook.

". . . as a sort of experiment," she said. "Maybe we can help Eddie get over his fear of workbooks."

At first Eddie was afraid of hurting Angela's feelings, but Angela told him she had gotten the answers wrong on purpose.

Miss Mason gave him a red pencil and Eddie crossed out all Angela's answers and filled in the right ones.

He worked very fast.

"Look what you did there!" Eddie said gleefully, making a big red X.

"I know," Angela said modestly.

"But here you put Freddy the Frog — and that is good," he said kindly, "because it is wrong. So you were right. But I think the workbook was trying to trick you into putting Susie the Snail, which is also wrong. Harry the Hippo is right, but I think you put the wrong wrong answer."

"That's right!" Angela agreed. "I got it wrong

for the wrong reason. Put two red X's," she suggested.

"I'm getting dizzy," Miss Mason muttered. "This has been the strangest week of my teaching career."

Sweet Potato Salad and Chocolate Graham Cake

On Saturday, June third, PINWHEEL POWER won first prize at the science fair. Nathaniel and Doug had been generous about sharing the credit.

A plaque on the side of the dollhouse read, BASED ON AN IDEA BY TINA STEELE.

Angela got credit, too. ADDITIONAL PAINTING BY ANGELA STEELE.

Miss Mason was at the fair.

"What a wonderful project," she said to Angela. "I understand that you helped, too."

Angela nodded.

"Is Tina here?"

"Yes," Angela said, "but she's in the locker room

fighting with her friend Melissa about camp."

There was a new crisis. Melissa had been telling everyone that the only reason Tina wasn't going to Camp Sunset was because she was in love with Doug and wanted to be with him.

"About camp?" Miss Mason asked.

Before Angela knew it, she was telling her teacher all about Tina and Nathaniel working at a camp and her parent's trip to Maine.

". . . but I don't want to go to Maine." Angela looked shyly up at her teacher. "I want to stay with you."

"What a lovely idea!" Miss Mason laughed. She put her arm around Angela. Then she leaned over and whispered, "I have a feeling that everything will work out."

Angela stared up at Miss Mason, her heart filled with joy. Not only did her teacher *want* her to stay with her, she had just said that everything would work out!

"I must speak to your mother," Miss Mason said. "Is she here?"

Angela was delighted. She took Miss Mason over to where her mother was standing and left them alone to discuss the plans for the summer.

When her mother had finished talking to Miss Mason, Angela pulled her aside.

"Did you and Miss Mason make all the arrangements?" she asked.

Her mother smiled. "Yes, it sounds like a wonderful idea. I said I would bring my sweet potato salad and, if I had time, a chocolate graham cake."

Angela thought it was very considerate of her mother to save Miss Mason from too much extra cooking when Angela went to stay with her.

At the end of the day, Miss Mason came over to say good-bye.

"You must be very good at painting," she said to Angela.

"Oh, I am," Angela said. "Do you need anything painted in your . . . um . . . home?"

Angela did not know if her teacher lived in a house or an apartment.

Miss Mason sighed. "There's always *something* that needs painting," she said.

That night Angela packed her blue smock in her suitcase so she could help Miss Mason with any painting that needed to be done.

* * *

On the last day of school, Angela's first-grade class had a picnic in the park. Meredith's mother made fried chicken and biscuits and Angela's mother brought her sweet potato salad and a chocolate graham cake.

Angela hoped Miss Mason wouldn't think that was all her mother could cook. She wondered if she should ask her mother to cook other things to take to Miss Mason's house.

But Miss Mason enjoyed the cake and salad so much, Angela decided she wouldn't mind having them all over again.

The picnic was fun. Angela had brought the temporary change-of-address card so Miss Mason could fill it out, but Miss Mason was never alone. She was always surrounded by parents and children.

Miss Mason kissed all the children good-bye and told them how much she was going to miss them. She told Angela the same thing, but Angela knew it was only because she did not want to show favorites. She did not want the rest of the class to know that Angela was staying with her that summer. It had to be a secret.

When they got home from the picnic, the house was in an uproar. Tina and Nathaniel were packing for camp. They were leaving the next morning.

Angela gave her mother the change-of-address card to fill out.

"But you'll only be gone for two weeks," her mother said. "I was going to ask the doorman to hold our mail."

"Not *my* mail," Angela said. "The post office has to know where I am. Besides, *I* might get something important."

Her mother laughed and said she would fill out the card just for Angela and give it to Felix.

The next morning Angela went to the train station with her parents to see Tina and Nathaniel off to camp.

The train station was a mob scene. Angela was sure she was the only child in the world who was not leaving for camp that day.

Tina, Nathaniel, and Doug were holding up signs so that their little campers could find them. Angela saw a mother introduce her little girl to

Tina. Tina leaned down to talk to her. A moment later, the little girl was jumping all over Tina. Tina was laughing.

Angela could not believe her eyes. Now Tina was giving the little girl a piggyback ride.

"But she's only just met her!" Angela tried to blink back the tears. Tina had not given Angela a single piggyback ride this year.

Tina had her hands full and so did Nathaniel. Angela watched as they led their campers through the gates to the train. They turned to wave, but Angela knew they had already forgotten her. New little brothers and sisters were taking her place.

"I'm just a leftover," she said to herself.

Angela felt very strange alone with her parents. As they left the station, her mother was sniffing back tears.

Her father put his arm around her mother. "Don't worry. They'll have a wonderful time."

Angela lagged behind. She was just testing her parents. She was testing them to see how many times they looked around for her.

They never did look around for her. They didn't even say, "Hurry up, Angela."

The apartment seemed silent and empty. Angela started a letter to Nathaniel.

Dear Nathaniel,
    I don't know if you remember me

It made her so unhappy, she never finished it. She removed the photographs of Tina and Nathaniel from her bedtable. It hurt too much to look at them.

Angela spent three mornings a week at a program at the hobby shop. She worked on presents for Miss Mason — a woven potholder, a painted plate, another potholder and another. . . . She packed these presents in her suitcase along with her stuffed animals.

Miss Mason had never seen her stuffed animals.

At five o'clock in the morning on the twenty-ninth of July, Angela climbed into the backseat of the rented car. There were suitcases and fishing rods on the luggage rack on the roof. She wondered how long it would take to get to Miss Mason's house. For some reason she had expected Miss Mason to pick her up.

The car smelled funny, and Angela felt drowsy. As the sun was coming up over a bridge, Angela fell asleep.

She woke up three hours later. They were driving on a highway.

"Are we lost?" she asked her mother. She was surprised Miss Mason lived so far away. How did she manage to get to school every day?

"Not at all," her mother said. "We're on the Massachusetts Turnpike." She handed Angela a sandwich.

Suddenly Angela sensed something was wrong.

"Where's the sweet potato salad?" she demanded angrily. "Where's the chocolate graham cake?"

"Oh honestly, Angela, I had enough work to do. You'll just have to make do with sandwiches and fruit. It will be hours before we get to Maine. We won't get to the Bluebird Cabins until after dark."

"Me, too?" Angela asked.

"Well, of course."

Angela gasped. "But what about Miss Mason?"

"What *about* Miss Mason?" her mother asked.

To Angela's ears, her mother's words sounded cruel. They sounded wicked.

Angela sat very still for hours and hours.

Her parents tried to get her to play some games. "What about animal, vegetable or mineral?" her father asked.

"No, thank you." Angela did not play games with people who tricked her.

They tried to get her to sing some songs, but Angela shook her head and clamped her mouth shut. She watched the entire state of New Hampshire go by and refused to count a single cow.

Angela only ate half her sandwich. She didn't feel like eating the rest. She pulled off little crumbs of bread and let them drop out the car window. She knew the birds would get them. She knew she could never find her way home, but she had to do something.

They crossed the border into the state of Maine. The forests got darker and darker, the trees closer and closer together, as they drove deeper and deeper into the northern woods. . . .

The Plot Unfolds . . .

The Bluebird Cabins had become run down over the years. There were twelve cabins, but Angela and her parents were the only people staying there. The rest of the cabins were boarded up.

From the steps of the cabin porch, Angela could look across the lake and see the modern cabins bustling with activity. There were children swarming all over the swimming docks and playing volleyball in a field.

"Maybe Angela would have liked it better over there," she heard her mother say. "There are so many children."

"It's completely filled up," her father said. "I

asked the owners. Besides, I have to admit I like it better here. It's so peaceful."

Her mother sighed. "I guess I do, too. We're closer to nature. Just listen to those frogs croaking."

Angela shuddered. Down below there was a big puddle almost the size of a small lake. It was covered with slime. The night they arrived her father had driven into it by mistake. The tires turned and turned in the mud. The car was stuck for an hour.

Angela had looked out the window of the car. In the car headlights she could see eyes popping out of the puddle. Hundreds of eyes. Eyes all over the place. It was a ghastly sight. Angela began to scream.

"They are just frogs," her father had said. "Quiet down, Angela."

Angela did not approve of anything in Maine. The stars were too big. The crickets were too noisy. The birds woke her up in the morning.

She refused to learn to swim. In fact, she wouldn't even put on her bathing suit.

She refused to make friends with a girl named Pamela who was the same age. Pamela was staying at the modern camp across the lake.

"Pamela seems like a nice little girl," Angela's mother said. "She wants to meet you."

"I don't like her," Angela said.

"But you haven't even spoken to her," Angela's mother said. "Why don't you like her?"

"I just don't."

One afternoon her father rented a motorboat so they could go fishing. Angela refused to fish. She sat in the boat wearing her life jacket and hummed little songs under her breath to warn the fish.

"Quiet, Angela," her father said.

Nobody got a single bite.

Angela moved up another few steps and strained her ears to hear what her parents were talking about on the cabin porch.

Angela's hearing had gotten quite sharp. She was always listening for clues. Why had her parents brought her to Maine? What were they planning to do with her?

"I didn't know Angela was afraid of so many things," she heard her father say.

"She never was afraid before," her mother said.

"If anything, she was too daring. Remember when she went off shopping by herself in the department store?"

"What's gotten into her?" her father asked.

"I wonder if we should . . ." Suddenly her mother's voice dropped so low, Angela couldn't hear anything.

It rained for the next two days. Her parents sat by the fireplace in the cabin reading. They offered to play card games with her. They offered to buy her a jigsaw puzzle and take her to the general store and buy her some ribbon candy.

"I don't feel like it," Angela said. She was now very suspicious.

On Friday evening the sun came out briefly, just before it set.

Angela and her parents had dinner on the screened porch. Angela put on her pajamas right after dinner and brought the stuffed animal she called Panda out onto the porch.

She lay in the hammock on the porch, holding Panda and pretending to be asleep.

Down below the frogs were croaking. She tried to erase the picture in her mind of that terrible puddle. She had to pay attention to what her parents were saying.

"We don't have a thing left to eat," she heard her mother say, "not even a slice of bread for tomorrow."

Angela found herself thinking those words had a familiar ring. Of course! They were straight out of *Hansel and Gretel.*

She couldn't hear what her father said, but a moment later she heard her mother's voice: "Now would be a good time to go. Angela's asleep. She won't even know we're gone."

Angela felt her mother tuck a blanket around her. She kept her eyes closed and tried to make her breathing sound regular.

"Maybe we should leave a note," her father said. "Just in case she does wake up."

"I guess that's a good idea. I'll get the flashlight and the knapsack. We can leave the car here and walk."

Angela heard her parents creep down the wooden steps. Their voices faded into the night.

She opened her eyes and leaped to her feet. She ran down the steps clutching Panda. She turned in every direction, but she couldn't see the light from their flashlight.

She had waited a moment too long.

Her parents had made their getaway.

Out of the Woods

The moon was bright. The sky was clear and filled with stars. The night wind whispered through the tops of the tall pine trees.

Jessica and Richard Steele could hear voices and laughter coming from the general store. Through the trees they could see lights from the windows and the smoke rising from the chimney in the moonlight.

On Friday night the general store was open late. It was a gathering place for the local fishing guides and for the families on vacation. It was the only store for miles around and also served as the local post office.

Jessica stopped and searched through her jacket pocket.

"I forgot the shopping list," she said.

"We don't really need it," her husband said. "Let's just pick up a few things and go right back to the cabin. I don't really feel comfortable about leaving Angela. We've already been gone ten minutes."

"I just wish she were having more fun," his wife said. "I still think we should invite Pamela and her family over for a cookout — even if Angela resists the idea."

Suddenly she grabbed her husband's arm.

"I hear something," she whispered.

"It sounds like an animal," Angela's father said, ". . . a wounded animal."

They both held very still and listened.

"I've never heard an animal cry like that," Angela's mother whispered.

Richard Steele shined his flashlight through the trees.

A small white figure was running through the woods. The child stopped short and froze like a frightened deer in the beam of the flashlight.

"It's Angela!" Angela's mother said.

Angela was wearing her white pajamas. She was barefoot and her feet and legs were covered with mud. She had stopped sobbing and held perfectly still. Then, suddenly, she saw them.

"You didn't fool me!" Angela shrieked at her parents. She was trembling with rage. "I knew the whole time. You tried to get rid of me, but *it didn't work!*"

She shook her little panda at them and shrieked accusations until she ran out of breath.

Her father lifted her up and carried her to the steps of the general store. Angela was panting. He cradled her in his arms, and whispered, "Calm down. Tell us what happened."

"Poor little lamb." Her mother sat next to them and stroked Angela's cheek very gently. "We never should have left you alone."

"Start at the beginning," her father said.

Angela gave her parents a look of profound mistrust, and began her story. She told them she knew they had been trying to get rid of her ever since she ruined Income Tax Day.

"What's so funny?" she asked when she saw them smiling at her.

"Oh, I don't know," her mother said. "I guess

I have trouble with the idea of 'ruining' Income Tax Day."

"It's not exactly our favorite day of the whole year," her father explained. "But, go on. . . ."

"Well, anyway," Angela said. "I was very bad so you forgot you had me, and then suddenly you remembered. So you and Mommy had to make a plan. . . ."

"A plan?" her father asked.

"Yes," Angela said, "a plan to get rid of me."

She suddenly noticed there were other people on the porch of the general store. She was quiet a moment.

"So," her mother went on, "we decided to take you into the Maine woods. . . ."

"*Deep* into the Maine woods," Angela corrected her.

"Yes, *deep* into the Maine woods and leave you there."

"That's right," Angela said. She thought it over. She let her father hug her tight. She let her mother stroke her cheek and call her "a poor lamb." She noticed that both of them were looking at her as if they loved her more than anything in the world.

Suddenly she didn't believe a word she was saying, but she had to go on. "You and Daddy waited and waited until just the right moment. As soon as you thought I was asleep, you sneaked away."

"But we were just going to shop for some groceries," her mother said. "We didn't want to wake you up."

"Ha!" Angela said. "So anyway, you crept away and left me all alone in the forest. . . ."

" . . . to be eaten by wild beasts," her father suggested.

"Yes." Angela was beginning to enjoy herself. "But that is not the worst thing you did."

"Wait a minute," her mother said. "You mean you *were* eaten by wild beasts?"

"Oh, yes," Angela said in a serious voice. "Five of them. And I was delicious. They are sitting on the porch of our cabin right this minute licking their chops."

Angela had to wait for her parents to stop laughing. Finally she burst out, "But listen to the worst thing you did! You made me run through the puddle with frog eyes in my bare feet!"

"How awful!" her mother said. "Did you really do that?"

Angela nodded. Suddenly she shuddered. She really *had* run through that puddle. She had run through it because she knew it led to the road.

"Did she really?" a small voice asked.

Angela turned her head.

"Well, hello, Pamela," Angela's mother said.

Angela scrambled out of her father's lap and stared at the little girl she had refused to play with — the little girl she had refused to even meet.

"Did you really run through that puddle?" Pamela's eyes shone with admiration. She looked down at Angela's muddy feet.

"Yes," Angela said shyly, "but I didn't step on any frogs. I think I must have scared them."

"Do you mind if I tell my brother?" Pamela asked. "I'll be right back."

A moment later Pamela was back. She was out of breath. "David wants to meet you. He's ten. He's inside playing with the kittens. Have you seen the kittens yet?"

"No," Angela said.

"Would you like to?" Angela's mother asked her.

"Yes," Angela said, "but I'm wearing pajamas."

"Silly!" Pamela said. "I'm wearing pajamas, too."

Pamela *was* wearing pajamas — light blue pajamas with little ducks on them. "It's okay," she assured Angela. "We're in Maine. No one will even look at you."

Pamela took Angela's hand and led her into the general store.

There were quite a lot of people in the store. A group of fishermen were standing around the wood stove arguing about fishing tackle and bait.

Pamela took Angela to the back where her brother David was sitting on a barrel playing with an orange kitten.

David had short blond hair that stood up straight and lots of freckles on his face. Pamela introduced Angela.

"This is the girl I told you about who ran through the puddle with frog eyes."

Angela was beginning to feel like a movie star.

Suddenly she felt a hand on her shoulder.

She turned around. Mr. Crooks, the owner of the general store, was standing behind her.

"Young lady. Tell your mother there's some important mail for her. Your mother's name *is* Angela Steele, isn't it?"

"No," Angela said. "I'm Angela Steele."

"Well, then there's some mistake," Mr. Crooks said. "There's a pile of mail waiting here for someone named Angela Steele, but it couldn't be for you. There are some letters from overseas and a package from the Internal Revenue Service."

"The Internal Revenue Service found me all the way up here?" Angela swallowed hard.

Mr. Crooks stared thoughtfully at Angela. He puffed on his pipe. Then he shook his head and went behind the counter. He reached into a cubbyhole and took out a pile of letters and a big envelope.

Angela stared at the official-looking envelope Mr. Crooks held out to her.

The general store had become quiet. Even the fishermen who were standing around the wood stove had stopped talking.

Angela suddenly found herself the center of attention. She heard one of the old-timers say to his friend, "Well, Clyde, how do you like that? Those feds must be getting pretty desperate. Imagine those tax people coming after a kid that size."

"The little girl?" Clyde asked.

"Yep. Tracked her all the way to Maine."

"The one in the white pajamas? Holding that panda bear?"

"Yep."

Clyde was disgusted. "Who will they pick on next?"

"Well, well, well . . ." Angela's father was standing next to her. "It looks as if the tax people finally caught up with you. It was bound to happen sooner or later."

Angela heaved a big sigh, handed her panda to her father and said to Mr. Crooks in her most grown-up voice, "I guess I'd better see what it says."

Angela opened the envelope from the Internal Revenue Service. She stared at the contents with a puzzled frown. Finally she gave up and handed the papers to her father.

Her father leafed quickly through them. He turned to Angela. "Angela," he said, "you got your money back." He turned to Mr. Crooks.

"You see, my daughter paid income tax this year. She gave the government every nickel she had. She was worried about the national debt."

Angela looked up at her father. He sounded proud of her.

"Is that right?" Mr. Crooks took another puff on his pipe.

"Yes," her father said. "And, believe it or not, she just got a personal letter from an agent of the Internal Revenue Service — a tax examiner named Violet Knight."

"I wouldn't have thought there *was* such a thing as a personal letter from the IRS," Angela heard Clyde grumble to his friend.

"Read it to me," Angela whispered.

Her father began:

"Dear Angela Steele:

The President of the United States forwarded your tax return to us. It came in the form of a Presidential Letter and, as such, it had to receive immediate and special attention."

Angela's heart was beating very fast. She had caused the government more trouble than she had ever imagined.

". . . but I'm afraid it took me quite a long time to find out how to handle your form, and I apologize for the delay. Although there is no place for your date of birth on the 1040 form, I guessed that you were a child — a generous and concerned child — a child of about my daughter's age, a third-grader, most likely. . . ."

Angela blushed with pleasure. Her father smiled at her and went on:

"Thank you for wanting to help, but it appears that you do not actually owe the government any taxes.

For that reason, we are returning your money in the form of a money order for $4.53. (Cash should never be sent through the mail.) But since you signed your 1040 form, it must be kept on file.

Enclosed is a booklet called "Understanding Taxes," which you may find interesting when you are a bit older.

Your form 1040 was beautifully dec-

orated. I know that you must have used your favorite stickers. (My daughter uses her rainbow stickers only for very special occasions.)"

Angela's face was bright red. "You can read me the rest of the letter later, Daddy," she whispered. "I've got to go back to the kitten."

"What about those other letters?" Pamela wanted to know. "Who wrote those?"

Angela shuffled quickly through her mail. "Let me see. Tina. That's my sister. Nathaniel, my brother. One from my grandmother, of course. Let me see . . . there's a postcard from Italy from my teacher Miss Mason. And . . . oh my goodness! There are two letters from Flor Elena . . . addressed just to me! Flor Elena is my orphan," she explained to Pamela.

Pamela looked very impressed. But Angela was getting tired of feeling so important.

"I can read my mail later," Angela said, and she took Pamela's hand.

About the Author

NANCY K. ROBINSON has written more than fifteen books for children, starting with a biography, *The Howling Monkeys: The Story of Ray Carpenter*, in 1973.

With *Wendy and the Bullies* in 1980 she switched to writing fiction and continues to win fans with each new book.

Angela, Private Citizen marks Angela Steele's third appearance in a Nancy K. Robinson book, following *Mom, You're Fired!* (where Angela makes her debut as a preschooler) and *Oh Honestly, Angela!*, which describes her life as a kindergartner.

In addition to writing, Ms. Robinson's special interest is photography. She has two children and lives in an apartment in New York City.